Paramedics

in

Stitches

by Penney Lang

Illustrations by Jane Farmer

Paramedics In Stitches

Edited by: Catherine Spain
Typesetting by: Roessler Graphics
Printed by: Roessler Graphics, Stanthorpe Qld. Australia
Book cover design: Penney Lang and Jane Farmer
Illustrations: copyright Jane Farmer in collaboration with Penney Lang

National Library of Australia Cataloguing-in-Publication data

Lang, Penney
Paramedics in Stitches
e-mail: parapen69@gmail.com

ISBN: 978-0-646-55190-6

Penney Lang

To my husband Dieter for his patience and ongoing encouragement.

Also to my parents Ray and Leesdia Trinder, who continue to put faith in me.

Paramedics In Stitches

Penney Lang

CONTENTS

Acknowledgements   9

Preface   11

Red Faces   15
1   Bad Hair Day   17
2   Toilet Trauma   20
3   Payback   22
4   Gear Glitch   24
5   Bouncing Back   26
6   Keyless Entry   28
7   Delicate Matters   31
8   Blue Day   34
9   Barney   37
10   First Impressions   38
11   Code Red   42

Recruits and Retirement   45
12   Forget-me-not!   47
13   Budding Paramedics   51
14   Thar She Blows!   54
15   High Flyer   55
16   Retirement of an Ambo   57

Travellin' Tales   59
17   Rock'n' and Roll'n'   61
18   The Reliever's Plight   66
19   Joy Ride   69
20   Army Duck   72

Never Work with Animals   75
21   Snake Charmer   77
22   Newsflash   80
23   Just Kidding Around   82
24   Stowaway   84
25   Kamikazes   86
26   Leapin' Lizards   89
27   Cat-astrophic   93

Radio Talk   95
28   Classic Comments   97
29   Ass No Questions   100
30   *Fawlty* Radios   102
31   Malfunctioning Mic   104
32   It Pays to be Honest   105
33   The Numbers Game   107
34   Wake-up Call   109
35   Piggy Questions   111

Practical Jokes   113
36   Toeing the Line   115
37   Microwave Biscuits   120
38   Town Crier   121
39   Goldilocks   124
40   Anybody for Takeaway?   128
41   Fish Food   130
42   Just Hangin' with the Gang   132
43   Handle with Care   135
44   Don't let the Bedbugs Bite   138
45   Long Way Home   140

Lessons Learned 143
46 A Duck in Time 145
47 Mr Snuggles 147
48 Fell off the Back of a Truck 149
49 Sweet Revenge 151
50 Hazardous Materials 154

Country Characters 157
51 Cheeky Challenge 159
52 The Ride 163
53 Outback Adventures 166
54 Country Music 168
55 Fine Talking 170
56 Outback Jack 172

Bits and Pieces 175
57 The Ripple Effect 177
58 Out of the Hearts of Babes 179
59 Supermedic 182
60 Fire! Fire! 185
61 When the Going gets Tough … 188
62 A Sticky Situation 192
63 Mamma Maria 194
64 Mind your P's and Q's 197

Seriously Now 199
65 Chicken Surprise 201
66 Skeleton Crew 205
67 Shocking Treatment 207
68 Perfect Timing 209
69 Booby Traps 211
70 Funny Faces 213

| 71 | A Really Big Boy | 215 |
| 72 | Trust me, I'm a Professional | 217 |

About the Author 220

Penney Lang

ACKNOWLEDGEMENTS

Special thanks go to Jane Farmer for her wonderful illustrations that inspired me to continue with this crazy idea.

For those who read over the first draft of my manuscript: Ray Trinder, Paul Nielsen and Peter Bulkeley. Thank you so much for offering your valuable time and your comments. You put me on track, which was what I needed, and there was no going back.

I would like to thank fellow author John Watkins who introduced me to my editor Catherine Spain. Our unexpected meeting that day paved the way for me to take this very important step.

Many thanks to Catherine Spain for guiding me through unchartered waters and going above and beyond what I expected, in more ways than one. You'll make an editor out of me yet.

And last of all, a big thank you to all my friends and colleagues who willingly shared their stories which helped me to make this project a reality.

Paramedics In Stitches

Penney Lang

PREFACE

During my career there is one question many people have asked: "What do you like most about being a paramedic?"

The obvious answer is: satisfaction from helping people. For me personally though, this job is also about boldly going where not many people are willing to go and at the same time having a few laughs. I love an adventure ... I'm married, after all.

It's not about how much gore one can stand or the number of cannulas and drugs given in the past week. It's about making a difference in someone's life, especially when there is a positive outcome. It's being the one person someone relies on when they need help; having the ability to give them 'time away' from that pain—physical or emotional; and making them smile.

Another common question is: "What's the worst you've ever seen?"

In an attempt to get out of remembering the trauma I *have* seen, I tactfully try to suggest to people that they really don't want to hear about the gore. But to those who are most persistent, I let them have it ...

"Well, you should have seen this motorbike versus truck accident I went to—what a mess! The motorcyclist was tangled up in the wreckage of his motorbike. He had one arm amputated, which was lying in the middle of the road. His face was covered in blood and he had a large gaping hole at the back of his head because the helmet came off in the accident.

11

I had a really hard time trying to untangle him from the motorbike, as his leg was caught up badly in the wreckage. His other arm was also broken with the bone sticking out. There was blood everywhere, you should have seen it! The only way I could untangle and treat him was to pull his leg free from the wreckage. So I pulled and pulled on his leg ... just like I'm pulling yours."

Being a paramedic isn't full of tragic times. The best jobs are the ones where you can create a more relaxed atmosphere in the face of adversity. There are also many circumstances where someone's misfortune puts a completely different view on an emergency call-out, as you will find out in this collection of short stories.

The following accounts are based on real events as far as I can remember, or my friends and colleagues can recall. However, all names have been changed and locations have been deliberately omitted to prevent any embarrassment and to protect the person's privacy. The exception to this is *The Reliever's Plight* that is based on actual locations.

Among the many paramedics with whom I have had the pleasure of working, some have stood out. Not necessarily because of their intelligence (they'll tell you differently of course) but because of their ability to bring a smile to many faces—especially mine. There have been many situations that have been out of the control of all of us.

I hope you enjoy reading these accounts as much as I have enjoyed remembering them.

So now I invite you to grab a cup of your favourite beverage, find a nice comfortable spot and enjoy the journey.

Penney Lang

Paramedics In Stitches

Red Faces

Paramedics In Stitches

1

Bad Hair Day

Many of the elderly people we treat these days smoked cigarettes in their youth, and now suffer from various respiratory ailments.

Unfortunately, bad habits are hard to break and we often find they cannot give up the cigarettes that have dominated their lives for almost half a century. Eventually they find they can no longer walk more than a few metres without supplemental oxygen, and so their whole life revolves around an oxygen cylinder.

When walking through the front door of the home of a patient suffering from a chronic respiratory illness, you can immediately hear the regular hissing sound coming from the portable oxygen concentrator. You are then greeted by the long trail of oxygen tubing, winding its way from one end of the house to the other, and, finally you see the point where it is attached to the patient.

At this stage in the patient's life, medical people hope to see the patient is no longer smoking. However, for some who have not been able to break the habit, there is one basic rule they must follow, especially when dependent on medical oxygen.

A crew was dispatched by the Communications Centre (Comms) one Friday afternoon, to a female patient who was oxygen-dependent.

When they arrived at the house, the paramedics were met by the patient's husband. He was leaning up against the wall of the house on the verandah, holding his stomach and laughing hysterically. He was absolutely speechless. When they asked him where the patient was, all he could do was point inside the house to where his wife was sitting.

As the paramedics entered, the smell of burnt hair filled their nostrils. In the lounge room, they found a female sitting in a recliner chair, still holding the charred remains of a cigarette between her fingers.

Her scorched and frizzled hair was blown away from her forehead, showing two white marks where her eyebrows had once been. With her face covered in black and slightly melted nasal prongs still inserted into her nostrils, the woman sat there blinking, with what was left of her eyelashes, and a look of bewilderment etched across her face.

The lessons from this story are:

1. Oxygen and lighters don't mix.
2. Paramedics need a good laugh, but not at the expense of the patient's health.

Talk about learning lessons the hard way. Maybe the Health Department should consider using the woman's image on cigarette packets to help deter smoking!

2

Toilet Trauma

Chris and his partner had just transferred a patient to the surgical ward, when they happened to walk past an elderly gentleman who was being assisted onto a commode.

Chris noticed that the elderly man had obviously undergone recent surgery to his throat, and his only means of communicating with the nursing staff was by using hand gestures and mouthing words.

As the nurse placed the pan in position, she hadn't noticed that it wasn't properly aligned with the relevant part of the male anatomy.

Chris could see an expression of discomfort on the elderly man's face indicating he needed help. A little while later, a matronly-looking nurse appeared at the man's side.

"Have you finished, love?" she asked in a sweet voice.

But before the man could indicate anything, the nurse started to pull the pan away from the commode, unaware that his testicles were caught.

Due to his inability to call out, the poor man shrieked in pain as the nurse pulled on the pan. With his eyes popping out of his head, blood vessels protruding from his temple and his face turning shades of bright red and purple, the man could only shriek and gasp in pain each time the nurse yanked at the pan, in an effort to dislodge it from the commode.

On seeing the poor man's plight, Chris came running to his rescue.

"STOP, STOP!" he yelled, holding up his hands.

Looking up at Chris, the man's eyes now overflowed with tears, grateful that relief was now imminent.

3

Payback

While I was a student I received a phone call from the Communications Centre Supervisor asking me to cover a sporting event the next day. It was called the 'All Blacks Carnival'. This was a football carnival for the Aboriginal and Torres Strait Islanders, an annual event known to be a bit rough. I declined at first but a very persistent supervisor talked me into it, with the usual sob story that he couldn't get anybody else. So when I finally agreed to do it he finished the conversation excitedly saying he owed me one.

Now let me tell you I was not looking forward to doing this event and had good reason to believe so.

Looking after two fields on my own brought the ridicule of those both on field and off field.

As the shade come in over the field in the afternoon, it became increasingly difficult to recognize somebody in trouble, as they all blended in with the shade.

While concentrating on a player who seemed to be injured on the second field, I hadn't noticed that another player, on the first field, was still on the ground and appeared to be injured. It seems the spectators forgot I only had one set of eyes. As a result, the commentator felt the need to call for the ambulance over the public address system, claiming that I was asleep. I had never been so humiliated before in my life and with each passing hour, twelve in all, I schemed and planned how to make **that** supervisor owe me BIG TIME!

And boy did I get him back. Two years later, I married him!

4

Gear Glitch

A young bloke, who hadn't been in the Ambulance Service for very long, attended a speedway event featuring both cars and motorbikes. Standing in the middle of the arena watching the motorbikes whizzing around the circuit, he felt his heart thumping hard against his chest as he waited in anticipation for one of the riders to come to grief.

He didn't have to wait very long. One of the bikes lost its grip in the dirt and slid into another rider, causing them both to crash into the side wall. As the young paramedic raced over to them, one rider was already on his feet, madly trying to kickstart the bike again and continue his race. However, the second rider gingerly stood up complaining of a hip injury. As the rider took the helmet off, the young paramedic was surprised to see that the rider was a female. After a quick assessment he ruled out any serious injuries.

"Why don't you come on over to the ambulance with me so that I can see what you've done to yourself?"

As he assisted the female rider over to the ambulance, he noticed she was wearing the proper bike riding leathers. Being a bike rider himself, he knew that these leather outfits were quite expensive. He also knew that she wouldn't be very impressed with him if he were to cut the leathers off just to examine her hip.

Being a professional young lad, he asked her, "Do you have any clothing on underneath?"

"Just my underwear," she replied.

Slightly embarrassed, he explained, "It's just that for me to examine your hip properly, you'll need to remove your leathers."

"Oh, that's fine," she laughed. "I'm not worried about you seeing *my* undies."

Before the young paramedic could open the back door of the ambulance to give her some privacy, the lady was beside the ambulance, taking off her gloves and unzipping her outfit.

"How about you hop in the back where you'll have a bit of privacy?" he suggested.

"No, don't worry about that. I don't think I'll be able to hop in anyway, because my hip's pretty sore." With that she continued unzipping her outfit.

Noticing that the patient was starting to struggle with the leathers, and obviously in a great deal of pain, the paramedic decided to assist her.

Facing the patient and kneeling down in front of her, he began to peel the leathers down. However, he didn't realize that, as he peeled the leathers down, the patient's underwear started to follow.

The poor young paramedic was frantically trying to pull the leathers down with one hand and at the same time pulling up the patient's underwear with the other while offering profuse apologies.

Thankfully the patient was very understanding. In fact, she was less embarrassed about the incident than the deeply blushing paramedic.

5

Bouncing Back

If you've ever had the opportunity to witness an ambulance arriving at the scene of an incident, you'll notice how the paramedics, after retrieving the necessary equipment from the ambulance, will *walk* to where the patient is located. They don't often run to the patient. This could be a bit confusing for bystanders who might be thinking: "This is an emergency. Why don't they hurry faster?"

The following account explains why.

After a quick assessment of a patient who was reasonably sick, I raced from the patient's residence to retrieve some equipment from the vehicle. As I ran down the couple of steps leading to the front lawn, I didn't see the moderately-sized hole, which was covered by long grass, near the bottom step. As my right foot went into the hole I could feel myself falling. I knew that if I put my left leg out in order to stop falling, I would end up hurting myself a lot more than I ultimately did. Therefore, I ended up doing a somersault on the patient's front lawn which must have looked really spectacular.

Nearby, a man and his wife were tending to their front garden. The man happened to look up just in time to see me fall to the ground.

"The ambulance officer has fallen over!" he

exclaimed.

As his wife stood up and turned in the direction he was pointing, the man dropped his gardening utensils and started to walk in my direction. But seeing me upright again, he then stopped in his tracks saying, "Nope, she's up again."

After rolling about on the lawn, I continued on toward the vehicle where my paramedic husband was getting some equipment.

"Did you see what just happened to me?" I asked him.

"No, what happened?"

"I just fell over at the bottom of the steps."

"Did you? And I missed it!"

So for the next few shifts I had to endure the cartoons and comments about my unsteady feet, my clumsiness and my drinking habits. The list goes on …

6

Keyless Entry

Legislation gives paramedics the authority to break and enter into premises or vehicles when it is suspected that a person is injured or unconscious inside. This authority is used only as a last resort when all other avenues of entry have been exhausted.

Bruce and his partner were dispatched to a two-storey block of units. They believed that there was an unconscious female inside. On arriving, the crew could see a few people had gathered at the front of the building. Alighting from the vehicle, they met a twelve-year-old boy who stated that his mother was locked inside on the top floor.

After searching around the unit and confirming that all doors and windows were locked, Bruce noticed the bathroom window on the second storey was open, and saw a drainpipe next to the window.

Confident he could climb up the drainpipe and into the window, Bruce started his ascent.

By now, the sight of the ambulance parked in the driveway and of Bruce doing this 'Batman thing' up the side of the building, had drawn quite a crowd of onlookers.

Reaching the window, he poked his head through and found an unconscious woman slumped on the toilet. Bruce thought for sure that the woman was dead. He needed to confirm his suspicions, but couldn't do it just by looking through the window.

Squeezing his bulky frame through, he landed with a thud on the tiled floor. The racket he made was enough to wake the dead. In fact, the noise aroused the woman from her unconscious state. When she moved, it frightened the life out of Bruce.

"What's going on?" was all Bruce could utter.

"I don't know," replied the woman looking up at him.

After some initial treatment, Bruce assisted the lady downstairs, explaining that they needed to take her to hospital.

As they walked through the sliding glass door of the unit, the woman's son emerged from the crowd, relieved that his mum was going to be all right. Digging his hands into his pockets, the boy walked in silence with his mum and the paramedics toward the ambulance.

As the woman settled herself on the stretcher, the boy suddenly pulled his hands from his pockets and asked, "Hey Mum, did you want these?" He promptly handed his mother the keys belonging to their residence.

7

Delicate Matters

Some of the cases paramedics get called to are just plain ridiculous, such as being called to an adult with a minor cut to a toe, or to someone who can't sleep. In direct contrast, some callers are panicking so much they don't give the full facts of what is happening. Consequently the case appears to be slightly ridiculous, but the request is still answered and an ambulance is sent.

In these situations, it is understandable that the paramedic would question the necessity for a call-out; that is, until they are actually on-scene and faced with the reality of the situation. An initial care factor of 'minus two' is quickly up-scaled to a 'ten plus', and sarcasm is soon replaced with empathy—especially in the following situation:

Two o'clock in the morning isn't the best time to be woken, let alone for a ridiculous job. This is especially true when, according to the nature of the case, it could be attended to at a more appropriate time—such as when the big yellow light has appeared in the sky. So you could imagine the 'joy' the paramedics felt when woken at this particular hour for a male patient who had a problem with a part of his anatomy.

When they entered the house, the paramedics could hear a male yelling out offensive language. They poked their heads around the corner to see a young man sitting in a lounge chair, yelling and pounding the armrests.

As the paramedics weren't impressed with the time of the call for a start, they were in no mood to tolerate a violent patient with a seemingly ridiculous problem. Going into defence mode, they informed the patient's wife that unless he settled down they would call the police.

When they said this, the lady replied that her husband wasn't a violent man, but was in a great deal of pain. This brought a change of attitude in the paramedics, but they needed to find out what had happened.

Reluctantly, and somewhat embarrassed, she explained to the paramedics that her husband's injury was the result of their very energetic love-making.

As Bill now approached the patient, his heart went out in empathy as the patient continued to grimace with unbearable pain. Bill crouched down next to him and said, "Mate, we know you're in a lot of pain, but we're going to have to take a look and see what's going on so that we can help you."

With that, the patient surreptitiously pulled the blanket away from his lap, revealing a sight that brought tears to the paramedics' eyes. Due to a ruptured blood vessel, the patient's appendage not only looked like a swollen, bluish/purple mass, but also appeared broken in half. They both cringed in disbelief.

"Oh mate!" the paramedics empathized together.

"Oh boy that's gotta hurt," replied Bill shaking his head. "I'm going to give you all the pain relief you need."

Consequently the patient spent three days in hospital.

8

Blue Day

On another occasion, the emergency call taker took a call from a very distressed man shouting, "I've broken it!"

"What have you broken sir?"

"My penis! It's broken in half."

"Oh dear," she said, trying to keep a straight face. "I'll get an ambulance to you straight away."

As I took the call from the dispatching officer, I thought to myself: Did I hear the message right?

The silence on the phone from my end prompted the dispatcher to give me more information.

I thought: Is this a joke?

Then I realized that these unfortunate injuries do occur. So, regaining my composure, I alerted my partner to the nature of the job.

Walking into the man's house, we sung out to inform him of our arrival. A soft groaning noise came from the back bedroom. Following the noise, we found the man curled up in the foetal position on top of his bed. Looking up at us he cried out in a feeble voice,

"It's broken."

As he pulled back his trousers revealing the swollen purple mass, my partner asked, "Are you in much pain?"

"No, not really. I've had a few of these," he said pointing to a number of heavy-strength beer cans lying on the floor.

"How many have you had?" I asked.

"Oh, probably about twenty this afternoon after finishing work."

With the patient's self-administration of his pain relief obviously working, we then took him to the hospital.

He stayed in hospital overnight waiting to be transferred to a larger hospital for surgery the next day. However, the patient elected not to have surgery so he discharged himself from hospital the next day and went home.

A couple of days later, the weather closed in and caused localized flooding in the town. This resulted in the closure of the man's workplace, leaving him with no other choice but to gather together with his friends at the local hotel. Some time later, after consuming a number of beers, the man happened to look down at his bare feet and discovered that they had become distinctly discoloured.

Panic had now set in among the man and his friends, as they thought the discolouration was associated with his previous injury. They bundled him up in their car and drove him to the hospital.

At the hospital the doctor was notified of the man's condition. Thinking the worst, that the man had developed a complication as a result of his earlier injury, the doctor dropped everything and raced in to the emergency room to where the man lay.

On closer examination, the doctor discovered that

the patient's discoloured feet was the result of the dye seeping from his wet, blue trousers—which had then stained his feet!

9

Barney

One paramedic, known as Barney because he resembled Barney Rubble from the *Flintstones*, finally decided to take the plunge and marry his longtime partner.

Choosing a date would be easy as they'd decided not to go on a honeymoon straight away. With that in mind, Barney figured he only needed one day off for his wedding.

Calculating the roster ahead to the month they wanted to marry in, Barney chose a weekend that he figured he would be on a rostered day off.

They were both looking forward to the big day and had everything organized. Or so they thought.

However, as the big day drew nearer, Barney found out, to his horror, that he'd read the roster wrong. Not only was he rostered on to work a day shift on the day of his wedding, but was also required to be on-call that night.

Poor ol' Barney spent a bit of time running around trying to find someone to swap a shift with him. Jokingly, no-one at the station would swap because they were all invited to a wedding on that day.

Mind you, someone had to swap for Barney, otherwise there wouldn't have been a wedding at all.

10

First Impressions

A reshuffle of the ambulance hierarchy meant that we were to get a new boss.

It was always customary that shortly after the boss had settled into his new position he or she had to do the rounds and meet all the staff in the area. A schedule was done up with a list of all stations that the new manager was to visit, which in turn was sent out to those involved.

It was always a pretty tight schedule and time was of the essence in ensuring that the trip ran smoothly and staff had enough time to meet the new boss.

The staff at one station had been busy preparing for the visit. Food and drinks had been arranged, the station was looking spick and span, and now it was just a question of waiting for their arrival.

John, who had been living at the station for a couple of weeks while on relieving duties, had been up all night attending to various cases. Although tired, he made the effort to wake in time for the visitors to arrive. Not expecting the entourage to arrive for another hour, John made his way to the combined locker and men's room. Before getting dressed, he left his freshly-cleaned uniform hanging up in the locker and, totally naked, John headed for the toilet cubicle with the morning newspaper tucked under his arm.

Without locking the door, he settled down to enjoy a moment's peace and quiet. It wasn't long however, when he heard muffled voices coming from the station's kitchen, and deduced that their visitors had arrived earlier than expected.

Suddenly John's solitude was broken by the words, "I'm just going to use your toilet."

Before John could reach up and lock the cubicle door, it was suddenly flung open by none other than the new boss.

As the man standing before him now gasped in horror, John could only do what any bloke would do in this situation. He calmly held out his hand, and with a big grin on his face said, "G'day, you must be the new boss. I'm John. Welcome to our station."

Dumbfounded by seeing the sight before him, the manager absent-mindedly took John's hand. After realizing what he was doing, he quickly released himself from John's grasp and bolted out of the locker room.

Looking pale and slightly shaken, the manager's companions became concerned for his health, asking him, "Are you all right?"

"Yes, I'm fine, but we are leaving *right now*!" he commanded.

"But I thought you needed to use the toilet," stated one of his companions.

"I can wait, but we are leaving *right now*!" repeated the manager.

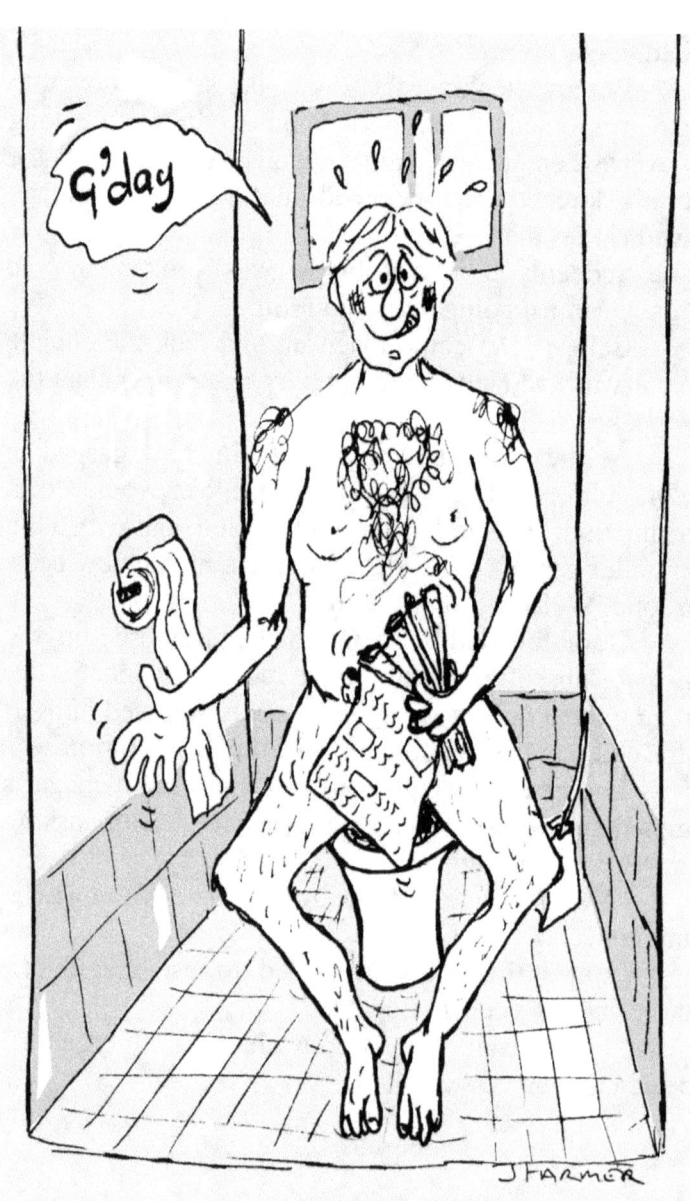

The visitors looked at each other, shrugged their shoulders and followed their leader out the door.

By the time John had emerged from the locker room, now fully dressed, he was surprised to find the visitors had left.

"What did you do to the boss?" asked one of John's colleagues.

Embarrassed, John told him what had happened.

Several months later, the boss attended another station to participate in a ceremony, where various members of the public had been invited.

After the ceremony, there was a barbecue. As the boss was about to tuck into a hamburger, someone asked him, "Have you met John?"

Looking up from his meal, the manager was startled as he recognised the familiar face before him. As visions of a hairy, butt-naked creature flashed into his memory, a smiling John said, "You remember me, don't you? We met a few months ago, I'm the toilet boy."

Turning a shade of crimson and struggling not to meet John's gaze, the manager looked down at his plate and stammered, "Yes, yes I remember you." Without looking up, the manager continued to finish his meal, trying to erase the vision from his memory, while ignoring the curious glances from other officers.

11

Code Red

Paramedics are not the only ones who face the start of each shift not knowing what the next eight to fourteen hours will bring. This mock incident report was made by one of the emergency medical dispatchers.

The ambulance control room can sometimes be an exciting place to spend part of a day. With many life-threatening situations being dealt with, and the amount of adrenaline pumping through everyone's body, anything is bound to happen.

It was one particular Friday that brought a different type of excitement:
It was noticed by a bored dispatching officer that a certain supervisor, who was German, had a slight defect in part of his uniform.

None the wiser, the fellow continued his usual antics, which included harassing staff and muttering to himself each time a problem appeared.

Finally, the dispatching officer had just about had enough, when the communications room ground to a halt with the cry: "Wolfgang, your fly is undone!"

Shrieking with embarrassment (which is hard to do

with a hamburger in your mouth), Wolfgang, who was now blushing a brilliant shade of crimson, made a grab for the offending apparatus and gave it a good tug.

Nothing happened!

Quick as a flash, he ripped off his 'strides' in full view of all and presented the staff with a view, hopefully never to be repeated, of parts of his body that had never seen the sun.

All modesty had departed and the staff were left with the sight of a very frantic man trying to revive a deceased zipper.

After a Code Zero (radio call for notification of a deceased patient) was declared, the trousers were transported via motorbike Code One (immediate response with use of warning devices normally on emergency vehicles) to a suburb nearby where they were hastily replaced with a healthier pair.

With Wolfgang's decorum and modesty finally restored, the shift somehow returned to normal.

Recruits and Retirement

Paramedics In Stitches

12

Forget-me-not!

For many years I had no clear ideas about what kind of career I would like to pursue—except that it should be challenging and worthwhile. After much encouragement from my family and friends, and especially from two particular ladies in the local St John Ambulance division, I finally decided, in 1991, to apply as a volunteer ambulance officer with the Ambulance Service.

After my first training night I felt confident that this was what I had been waiting for. Watching the US television show *Emergency!* in the afternoons after school must have planted a seed, as images of Roy DeSoto and John Gage responding to all types of emergencies in squad 51 all came flooding back, and I found myself keen to join the ranks of this respected profession.

At that particular time I worked part-time in a pet shop, but three times a week I would work an eight-hour shift at the ambulance station, on a voluntary basis, clocking up my hours and receiving invaluable training in the process.

The following year I was invited to attend my first block of training. This was four weeks of tuition in basic pre-hospital care, and formed the first block of the

Associate Diploma of Applied Science (Ambulance), with the majority of students in the same situation as me—eager to get into full-time work.

After successfully completing this training, I was eligible to apply for most ambulance officer positions around the state. At this stage, the minimum qualification for an ambulance officer position consisted of the first block of training that I had just completed.

At first I was a bit selective in applying for the positions that came out in the Ambulance Service weekly gazette, but as I grew keener and more and more impatient, I then started applying for more. I was so determined to get a full-time position, in the end I would scan the weekly gazette and apply for every position that I could—even if I had never heard of the place before, let alone know where it was in Australia.

I had a pretty good system going, as my resume remained unchanged with each position. I only had to change the name of the station I was applying for and send along an additional three copies. Therefore, it wasn't unusual for me to apply for five positions at once. As I made the additional copies for each application, I jokingly said to the officers, "They'd better give me a job soon, because either the Ambulance Service is going to go broke supplying photo-copy paper, or they're going to get to know me *really* well at State Headquarters and the Recruiting Office (both of which were in the same building).

Two interviews and thirty-six applications later, I received a phone call from the Ambulance Service on a day that I happened to be working at the pet shop. The officer informed me that they wished to conduct a telephone interview with me later that morning for one of the positions I had recently applied for. Excitedly I agreed to be available at the time nominated for the telephone interview.

My current boss was aware that I was keen to join the Ambulance Service, so I informed him of my interview for that morning. I figured that at the time of the interview my
boss would be in the shop to serve any customers and I wouldn't be disturbed during the interview. But he had other things in mind.

About half an hour before my interview, my boss informed me he had an appointment to go to that afternoon, and therefore requested me to go to lunch early. Realizing I would miss the phone call while on my break, I decided to return to work earlier, in time for the interview, while my boss was still there.

As soon as I walked in the door, my boss suddenly said, "Oh good, you're back early, so I'll head off now."

With my plans now completely destroyed and panic mode starting to set in, I decided I had to make the shop a priority, even if that possibly cost me the interview. Not five minutes after my boss left, the phone rang.

After explaining the interview process, the officer conducting the interview asked if I had any questions. I informed the interview panel that I was at the shop on my own and if I had a customer I would have to interrupt the interview and serve them.

The officer agreed to this saying, "Well, if you need to interrupt the interview, just let us know."

The interview went well. I can confidently say though, that I would be the only person in Australia who has sold a bird cage and a variety of other pet food and accessories during an interview for the Ambulance Service.

Many months later, I received a letter stating that I had been selected for the position. Finally, I was leaving home and on my way to start a new career.

It wasn't long after I had settled in at my new station, when we received a visit from some hierarchy from the Ambulance Service headquarters.

As my officer in charge introduced me to these men, one officer mused out loud, "Penney ... Trinder ... I've heard of that name before."

With a broad grin on my face, I shook his hand and thought to myself: I'm sure you have sir, I'm sure you have.

13

Budding Paramedics

One of the most enjoyable experiences I've had throughout my career so far has been working with student paramedics. They are so keen and eager to learn, and enthusiastically jump with anticipation every time the phone rings, hoping it's a 'lights and siren job'—only to have their hopes dashed when the emergency medical dispatcher asks for a roster. All of the students I have mentored have been an absolute pleasure to work with.

In some metropolitan stations there are several crews rostered on for the night shift. Sometimes the nights are slow and are were ample opportunities for rest. One officer always made me laugh—and still to this day a smile creeps on my face—as I recall a peculiar routine he would perform whenever asleep and the phone rang.

I must confess that whenever people get the fright of their lives, watching their reaction just cracks me up. It doesn't matter how intelligent or sophisticated a person is, whenever one gets a fright, all composure, self-confidence and intelligent speech is replaced by meaningless babble. If you're really lucky, you may also see their arms flap and their eyes dilate to the size of dinner plates.

Rick, on the other hand was different! The incomprehensible speech was evident but, whenever the phone rang, he would always perform this unusual but often humorous act. Once this happened, I would find it extremely difficult to answer the phone.

The setting is a typical night shift, and all is quiet. Rick is fast asleep. Suddenly the phone rings. While I get up to answer it, Rick is busy having what a non-medical person would presume was a seizure. With arms and legs flailing about in all directions, he resembles someone drowning or attempting to fly. I could never be quite sure.

In reality, though, Rick is quite the acrobat. If the Olympics ever included 'bed acrobatics' in the gymnastics event, he would win gold for sure. In fact, he tells me he's choreographed the whole event and never misses a beat and calls it his 'triple somersault with pike and twist'. I bet the diving team couldn't beat that one!

The state of the bed and sheets after this energetic display looked like the remains of something the cat had scraped up and buried. I do feel sorry for his wife these days when Rick is on-call at home, as I believe nothing's changed.

14

Thar She Blows!

One student paramedic copped a lot of ribbing from his peers, due to an incident involving the ambulance at another station where he was relieving.

Intending to wash the ambulance at the end of the day, he drove the car out of the plant room (where ambulances are parked at the station), and backed it into an area beside the plant room. However the fuel storage tank, which had been recently filled, seemed to get in the way.

He discovered that backing into and rupturing a storage tank can cause a bit of a problem. Spilling 2500 litres of fuel caused all sorts of major dramas, not to mention the cost of the fuel. Suddenly, the town was woken from its sleepy state as many other services and government agencies took more than a casual interest in the proceedings. One beneficiary of the spillage was the pub, which never had so many patrons.

The end result, after the cleanup, was lots of paperwork, including: the vehicle damage report; environmental protection agency report; insurance reports relating to the damage of the ambulance building; and many other forms.

The student later remarked that he never had a dull moment during the rest of his relieving period at this station.

15

High Flyer

Attending the Motocross can be a very dirty and noisy time. At one particular Motocross park there were two tracks—the hilly track and the flat track. The flat track was great for the little ones riding their 50cc bikes, which sounded like a swarm of mosquitoes ready to invade as they rode past.

The hilly track included many jumps and turns for the more experienced. The sight of motorbikes and their riders flying over some of these jumps was quite spectacular and the skill of the riders was something else.

On this particular day, both tracks were running and an experienced paramedic, along with a young female student paramedic, had the privilege of attending this event. The experienced paramedic had seen most of the thrills and spills that are common in Motocross events, but reckoned this incident took the cake.

While treating a young rider for injuries resulting from an awkward landing, the paramedic asked his colleague to bring the ambulance over to that location.

In the near distance, the paramedic could hear the ambulance coming across the paddock. This was soon replaced by sounds of gasping coming from the crowd that was then replaced with the distinctive loud sound of the ambulance revving.

The paramedic looked up in time to see the undercarriage of the ambulance coming up over the same jump that the young rider had just come to grief on.

16

Retirement of an Ambo

I started writing poems while in my mid-teens. I must have been the only kid in class who actually liked poetry and, over the years, have found it a satisfying and challenging way to express myself about nature and the people I have met along the way. Therefore I decided to add a few poems to this compilation of short stories.

Retirement Of An Ambo came about when I had not long started as a student ambulance officer in 1993.

I was fortunate enough to have spent some time with a particular officer who had obviously spent quite a large part of his life attending to the needs of the community where he lived.

It was quite obvious, from the first time I met him, that he really loved the job. Unfortunately age had caught up with him, and so his retirement date was approaching rapidly.

It is people like this, who are so dedicated to helping their fellow man, any Ambulance Service in the world would be proud to have on their team.

It is truly a shame that age gets in the way of something you love.

Retirement of an Ambo

The Service is losing one of their best,
For Ol' Mate's leaving the ambulance nest;
"I've finally come to the end of my game,"
But things will never be quite the same.

He's been an ambo for many years,
Transporting patients and the old dears;
Losing his glasses he's bound to do,
And blames anyone just passing through.

While at work he's there with a grin,
Additions to your car you know where he's bin;
Ten cases completed he never lingers,
But counts only eight on remaining fingers.

To those like Ol' Mate who've got a big heart,
Don't think at all you've not played your part;
You've helped so many but the time has now come,
Retirement awaits and your work is now done.

Travellin' Tales

Paramedics In Stitches

17

Rockin' and Rollin'

When the paramedics received the job, it sounded like a routine call-out to the shipping port. Karen and her partner were called to standby at the pilot station where an injured male patient was said to be coming in by police launch from a catamaran situated out past the harbour.

Soon after, however, the police called through on the radio stating that the patient's injury was worse than they initially thought and they now needed the paramedics to come out to the catamaran. A pilot boat was then commandeered to transport the two paramedics.

The weather conditions were not favourable and it was rough enough inside the harbour, let alone out on the ocean. As the pilot manoeuvred the boat past the coastal headlands and through the six-metre swell, Karen anxiously looked at the pilot for some sort of reassurance that the little vessel they were in would handle the rough conditions.

However, the pilot's demeanor didn't help. He had one hand on the wheel and was casually chomping on a sandwich, as if they were on a Sunday afternoon cruise through the mediterranean. This didn't help Karen's physical and emotional state as, apart from being scared to death, the slight nausea she had felt earlier took a turn for the worse and she was now feeling quite seasick.

On mentioning this to the pilot, he motioned to the crew for Karen to be taken out of the enclosed cabin to the back of the boat. Here she was strapped securely into what looked like a baby's harness and hooked up to the rails on the back deck so that she wasn't washed overboard.

After half an hour of crashing up and down over the choppy six-metre swell, the crew and her partner came to let Karen know that they were not far from the catamaran.

At this stage a dishevelled and nauseated Karen lifted up her head.

"He'd better be crook," she slowly muttered. Then she turned to her partner saying,

"You'd better treat him because I don't want to look at him. I am wet, cold and sick. Actually, I don't want to see him—at all!"

Suddenly the radio crackled to life. It was the police saying that the male on board wasn't injured and was now on the police boat with the catamaran being towed behind. As Karen tried to control her anger she muttered to herself, "This man doesn't realize just how lucky he is."

She soon felt slightly relieved that at least they could turn around and head back to dry land. Or so she thought.

The pilot had earlier been notified of a cargo ship waiting to be escorted into the shipping port.

"But can't you drop us back first?" pleaded Karen.

"Sorry, but no. We have already lost time in being diverted to the catamaran," replied the pilot.

With that he put the boat back into gear. Once again they charged through the grey and white angry ocean, which tossed them about like a wine cork in a washing machine.

Karen's white knuckles clenched the harness enveloping her, while her stomach gurgled and churned like the hungry sea below. She closed her eyes feeling the continuous spray of salt water against her face and body as the giant waves continued to crash around them. As the little pilot boat lurched from side to side, it slowly made its way toward the cargo ship.

Finally, after enduring this treatment for what seemed like a never-ending nightmare, Karen could feel the pilot boat start to slow down. It no longer crashed into the waves but now took on a nauseating rocking motion. Eventually she felt a shadow descend on her.

Drenched to the skin, her hair plastered all over her pale face, Karen slowly opened her eyes. Peering through her bedraggled and dripping hair she saw a grey metal wall. Confused as to what this was she started to say, "What the ... " However, Karen's words were cut short as her eyes slowly followed the large metal hull upwards.

Bending her neck back as far as it would go, with mouth agape and eyes widening, she mouthed the words, "Oh ... my ... goodness."

Looking straight up into the sky she could see what appeared to be many Asian men peering over the side and looking down at her from the huge ship that dwarfed the tiny pilot boat.

As the pilot ascended the narrow rope ladder of the cargo ship, Karen settled back in her harness and readied herself for the slow traumatic roller-coaster trip back to dry land.

Finally, her journey came to an end. With her land legs back, a nauseated, cold, wet and bedraggled Karen climbed into the ambulance, where her partner administered some oxygen and transported her back to the ambulance station where they were stood down for the rest of the shift. Miraculously though, Karen never lost the contents of her stomach during the entire sea voyage.

These days, Karen has classed herself as being a landlubber and has vowed never to go on a boat again. She has since moved as far from the ocean as possible—to the outback. However if some well-intentioned person does invite Karen to go for a 'lovely boat ride', they suddenly find themselves confronted with a pale, head-shaking and very nervous Karen who tells them politely they can go for a 'lovely boat ride' all by themselves.

18

The Reliever's Plight

Ambulance Services often employ some officers to work as relievers. They are qualified paramedics who relieve the permanent officers who are away at training, meetings or annual leave. These paramedics may find themselves relieving at a number of different stations within a fortnight.

I spoke to a number of relievers in south-west Queensland who told me of their experiences.

Hence in September 2007, *The Reliever's Plight* made its way onto the printed page.

Penney Lang

The Reliever's Plight

I wake in the morning to see where I'm at,
Am I in Roma or even Surat?
A bed I'm not used to, I've had a bad night,
'Cause this is the tale of a reliever's plight.

So here I am in Meandarra,
Off the beaten track, but close to Tara;
The lack of people might be off-putting,
But I'll have some work if Huey's cooking.

The phone is ringing, could be the one,
Not somebody please who weighs a big tonne;
Nor one who's drunk or some little monster,
No it's just Comms who want a new roster.

I pray to God, I'm really pleading,
Send me home, I hate relieving;
Don't leave me here in this town that's bare,
I really hate it when they just stop and stare.

Another weekday and I'm on the go,
Surat's as old as Cobb & Co;
They tell me later that there's no doctor,
For some help I'll call in the local copper.

The clouds are coming, it's like a sauna,
Here's my chance for a little trauma;
It's started to rain so run for cover,
A few moments later, and it's all over.

Next they tell me I'm off to Wandoan,
Where the flies are bad and the wind is blow'n';
Not to mention those slithery creatures,
Just one of this town's more common features.

It's on the increase so they say,
They're building up the old railway;
The mines are opening for the better,
It won't break the drought or make it wetter.

The months go by and all too soon,
I'm in the office and at Taroom;
The town is friendly, there's lots to see,
Down the road is Leichhardt's tree.

The town sign reads, 'Thank you for calling,'
I'm glad my car didn't end up stalling;
My journey has started, to home I am nearer,
The best view though, is the rear-view mirror.

In the morn I wake, to myself I'd say,
"Where on earth have I woken today?"
But as I look around, I don't have to dread,
I'm home on days off and goin' back to bed.

19

Joy Ride

The introduction of helicopters into the Ambulance Service allowed paramedics to reach people in remote locations easily, therefore to providing quicker transport to hospital. In the initial stages, there were only a few paramedics specifically tasked for aero-medical evacuations. However, if you happened to be on shift when none of these officers were available and a case came in that required the use of the helicopter, one might have taken the opportunity with both hands.

Such was the case one afternoon when a call came in to retrieve a patient from one of the resorts on an outlying island.

Jack and I just happened to be at the airport, after completing another job, when we were notified of the case. Jack was beside himself with elation at the prospect of going in the helicopter. He had been waiting for this moment for absolute months and had been training every day, either swimming or running, to eventually be selected to work in the helicopter full time. He was even receiving swimming lessons in an effort to improve his timing.

There was one problem though—only one paramedic went on the helicopter. During Jack's joyous moment, where he revelled in an odd little dance routine,

I didn't have the heart to burst his bubble that I was also keen to go on this case. Then I think it hit him. Turning to me with a serious look on his face he asked, "Did you want to go?"

"Well I wouldn't mind Jack," I replied.

"How 'bout we toss for it then?" he suggested. I agreed that this would be a fair thing.

As the coin flipped in the air, I called, "Heads."

It was a beautiful day for flying. The brilliant blue ocean mirrored the sky and clouds. As I looked out over the tropical islands, I could see the beautiful white sandy beaches glistening below. As we neared our destination, the palm trees swayed gently in the tropical breeze around the resort buildings.

Landing near the resort, we located our patient, who was waiting for us in a building not far from the landing pad. After treating the patient and loading him into the helicopter, we made the twenty minute flight back to the mainland.

I'll never forget the look of disappointment on Jack's face as his hand, which had been covering the coin, slowly revealed the queen's head. Poor Jack. I did feel a bit sorry for him, but as he pointed out, he would have an opportunity another day.

He was right. Jack eventually went on to become an intensive care paramedic and would have the opportunity of numerous flights to many of the islands and communities surrounding the area he worked.

20

Army Duck

The area in which I worked had just experienced the worst flooding in many decades. In just a few hours the water had suddenly invaded many homes, leaving many people stranded. Public buildings, such as the cinema, provided emergency shelter for those who had gone to the movies, but were unable to return home.

The next morning, my husband and I received a call from the communications manager informing us of the disaster, and our only means of transport to work that morning was by an army truck.

My partner Chris and I worked out of an army ambulance that day which also came with an army driver. This vehicle had the clearance to reach most destinations, and although the weather was dreadful I was grateful to have some experienced defence personnel on board with me (Chris was ex-army).

We were dispatched Code One to a patient suffering chest pain. Driving along one of the main roads, lights flashing and siren blaring, we came across a dip in the road with close to a metre of water flowing quite freely across it. Without thinking twice, the army driver drove the ambulance straight into the fast flowing river before us … and then it stopped!

There in the middle of this raging river, with

water pouring through the vents in the dash, my feelings of security and confidence in the Defence Force were suddenly floating away, as was the vehicle we were in. With panic in our voices we urged the driver to get us out of our current predicament.

I'm not sure if it was the tone of our voices; the feeble attempt of a sad siren trying to be heard underwater; or the sight of the Channel Nine News crew pulling up across the road that did it; but suddenly the engine spluttered back to life and we were out of there!

Penney Lang

Never Work with Animals

Paramedics In Stitches

21

Snake Charmer

Living behind the ambulance station in outback Australia had both advantages and disadvantages. One particular day my husband, who was the officer in charge, was on a day off but decided to walk down to work with me and have a chat and a cup of coffee with the other staff members on duty for that day.

I walked down the path from our house and through the gate first, followed by my husband, who was wearing a cap, t-shirt, shorts and thongs.

As he walked through the gate, he felt something brush up against his leg. Thinking it was the cat, he looked down and saw a snake chomping on his ankle. Lifting up his leg, he found that the snake clung to his ankle and wouldn't let go. Flicking his leg back and forth, he finally managed to shake the snake off his ankle.

Meanwhile … I was putting some rubbish in the bin when I heard him start to shriek.

With my back turned to him I thought to myself: What on earth is he going on about?

"Snake, snake!" he started yelling.

At this stage he had my attention. I whipped around and saw the snake, which was about a metre long, slithering away to the bushes nearby.

"Good thing it didn't bite you," I said.

"Yes it did," he replied. "It bit me!"

After I had treated my husband and transported him to hospital in the ambulance, it was confirmed that he had been bitten by a brown snake. He spent two days in hospital before he was allowed to come home.

For months later, when anything moved or touched his leg, my husband would jump and shriek at the same time … reminding me of one of those cats in a cartoon that gets a fright and ends up clinging to the ceiling above.

On one occasion, as we were travelling up the highway to attend to a patient, the radio microphone cord brushed up against his leg.

It is definitely **NOT** a good thing for the passenger to see the driver trying to alight from a moving ambulance at eighty kilometres per hour, screeching incomprehensible words, with both hands flapping in the breeze!

22

Newsflash

Residents of a small community awoke one morning to see a paramedic frantically taking his uniform off in the front yard of his residence.

Apparently, the feline member of the family had caught a mouse and brought it inside the house to show off her catch.

Leaping into action, the paramedic managed to rescue the little rodent from the cat's jaws, but soon lost his grip. The mouse took advantage of this and escaped inside the long sleeve of the paramedic's overalls. At the direction of his wife, the paramedic was soon outside and descending the flight of stairs at the front of the house, with one cat in hot pursuit.

Once at the bottom of the stairs, all attempts to retrieve the mouse from the sleeve failed, as the mouse had now moved to higher ground ... travelling up the paramedic's arm and onto his shoulder. The rodent then continued down his back and found a comfortable spot in the seat of the paramedic's pants. At this stage, the paramedic was hastily unzipping the front of his uniform, pulling it down to his knees.

Finally, after experiencing quite an adventure in its temporary hiding place, the little rodent scrambled out of the bottom of the trouser leg and escaped to a safer hiding place.

Having exposed most of his body to the community, the paramedic, now relieved from mouse duties, re-dressed himself and resumed his morning activities in getting ready for work.

23

Just Kidding Around

On one extremely hot afternoon, Adam and I were sent to a man who had fallen from a roof. As we made our way to where the man lay, we walked along a narrow path between the house and an in-ground pool—which on this day was very inviting.

As I approached the man, I saw that he obviously had a fracture to the arm. Leaving his arm in the comfortable position that it was, I began to assess the patient's head for signs of other injuries. As I separated the man's hair to examine his scalp, I was surprised to find I was not looking at his scalp, but at what appeared to be some kind of netting. Then it dawned on me that the man was wearing a toupee.

While I was regaining my composure from my surprise and embarrassment, the pet goat, which had been in the backyard nibbling at the ambulance response kit through the fence, suddenly appeared at our side and headed for the patient.

Adam leapt up and chased the goat back around to the front of the house. Suddenly we heard a great splash!

As I continued to treat the patient and wondered who had fallen into the pool, the goat came skidding around the corner on the tiled surface. With its four legs splayed out doing a poor imitation of *Swan Lake*, it headed toward us, dropping 'nuggets' everywhere, soaking wet and obviously very distressed.

After we had barricaded the goat in the backyard and delivered our patient to the hospital, I asked Adam, "How on earth did you manage to get the goat out of the pool?"

"The goat was well and truly underwater. Actually it was standing on the bottom of the pool looking up at me," explained Adam. "It was starting to gurgle at this stage, but came up for one last gasp of air. As the goat did so, I grabbed hold of its horns with one hand and hooked my other arm around its neck, and hauled it out of the water."

Another life saved … all in a day's work.

24

Stowaway

On another occasion, a call came in one night for the ambulance to attend a patient on a property which was a long way from town. With the patient on board and Jim, the officer in charge treating, they made their way back to town on a corrugated dirt road.

Every now and then Jim could hear a banging or thumping noise. Leaning into the front compartment he asked his partner where the noise was coming from.

Apparently, kangaroos were everywhere. Despite the driver's attempts to avoid hitting them, he did collect the odd one. They were even running into the side of the vehicle as it drove along.

After arriving at the hospital and handing the patient over to the hospital staff, the paramedic who had been driving signaled to Jim to come outside.

"Come and have a look at this!" he exclaimed.

There, in the driveway of the hospital, was a kangaroo carcass.

"We must have dragged that thing at least sixty kilometres," said Jim. "I'll see what I can do about it."

Walking back inside the hospital, Jim went up to one of the nurses and asked, "Can I have a body bag please?"

"What do you want a body bag for?" she asked

with a confused look on her face.

"I need it for a body," replied Jim smugly.

"You haven't got a body!" retorted the nurse.

"Yes I have; come and see for yourself," he replied in a more serious tone.

A look of shock came across her face as she now realized Jim wasn't joking. Shaking her head she whispered, "I'm sorry, I didn't realize you had a body as well," and promptly retrieved a body bag for him.

As the nurse walked outside, she could see the two paramedics standing over something in the driveway. As she got closer her eyes widened. With mouth agape, she pointed to the mangled carcass on the ground and exclaimed, "That's a kangaroo's body!"

"Told you we had a body," laughed Jim.

25

Kamikazes

The country was still in the grips of a severe drought, which meant the kangaroo population out west were on the move in search of food. Unfortunately, they would often come to grief with the passing traffic, as the only green grass to be seen for kilometres was on the edge of the roadway.

In October 2007 while I was on my way to another station for relieving duties, I noticed there was quite a large number of kangaroo carcasses on the side of the road.

Even in the middle of the day, I have witnessed several bounding across a paddock and then leaping through a barbed wire fence without letting up. At other times, they have leapt from the bush at full speed, straight onto the roadway in front of me, and kept going.

I thought: It was no wonder so many had come to grief—they have no road-sense. In a way, they're all Kamikaze roos.

Hence, a poem started to emerge, and by the time I had reached my destination, *Kamikazes* had been written.

Penney Lang

Kamikazes

They hide in the shadows, can't see if one's there,
The golden rule is, where there's one there's a pair;
You're careful and watching all that you do,
Mind you don't meet a Kamikaze roo.

One jumps out, then two, three and four,
My goodness there must be a dozen or more;
A barbed wire fence, they all stumble through,
All too close for a Kamikaze roo.

A tourist on a bus exclaimed, "That's a whopper!"
The bus driver grinned 'n' said, "That's our grasshopper."
"But he came out so fast, just out of the blue,"
It was none other than a kamikaze roo.

The birds are well fed here in the outback,
Especially the crows that grow really fat;
Perched on a skeleton, a bird or two,
The last remains of a Kamikaze roo.

A certain smell wafts through a nice little town,
The blokes on the seat look together and frown;
For there under the car, it cannot be true,
It's draggin' along a Kamikaze roo.

A traveller complained of dead roos on the roads,
"Don't kill your icon as if they were toads."
"Sorry," he said when he came back on through,
"I couldn't avoid that Kamikaze roo."

There stands Big Red the size of a man,
The Wallaroo, small, with fur of dark tan;
Try miss the Pretty Face whatever you do,
Whatever the breed, it's a Kamikaze roo.

Mum stops at the butcher's to have a good look,
"I'll get some advice on what I can cook."
"Wanna try something different, hey this one is new."
And hands her a packet of Kamikaze stew.

26

Leapin' Lizards

What possessed a female paramedic driving an ambulance on the highway to suddenly come to a screaming halt, frantically pull out the two stretchers, and proceed in belting the life out of the floor with a wheel brace?

1. Did the floor of the ambulance need some panel work done?
2. Was there a member of the animal kingdom let loose in the back?
3. Did the attendant's chair become loose from being anchored to the floor?

Or

4. Was she suffering from a 'fight or flight' response?

Our body's reaction to a sudden stressful situation, triggers off a chemical reaction involving a number of nerve cells. These cells fire off causing a number of chemicals, such as adrenaline, to be released into our bloodstream resulting in a syndrome called the 'fight or flight' response. The chemicals released prepare our body for either fighting the source or fleeing from it.

Sharon was asked to travel to another rural

ambulance station to relieve there for a week. After about twenty minutes into her journey she felt something move across her legs. Thinking that something had fallen from the passenger seat, where she had placed some of her belongings, she bent down to move it away from her legs. However, as she started to bend down, she felt the 'object' move over her boots, through her legs and then under her feet. Looking down she saw a huge brown snake slithering around her legs.

This is where the 'fight or flight' response began.

The Flight:

As Sharon slammed on the brakes she locked the wheels up causing smoke to billow out from the back tyres and finally managed to pull the vehicle over to the side of the road. Before the vehicle had come to a complete halt, she flung the door open and leapt out— still holding onto the radio microphone.

With the microphone cord stretched to its limit, Sharon's hysterical voice was heard throughout the entire region as she screeched into the mic, "There's a snake in the car. There's a snake in the car!"

Meanwhile, back at the station, Glen was sitting in the kitchen having a coffee, when suddenly he heard a commotion coming over the two-way radio. Alerting the officer in charge that their female colleague appeared to be in some sort of trouble, they started to listen to the radio message but couldn't quite make out what she was saying. She was talking very fast, in an excitably high-pitched tone.

Looking at each other the officer in charge said, "Is she saying there's smoke in the car or a snake in the car?"

"I don't know," replied Glen shrugging his shoulders.

"Come on then," said the officer in charge, "let's go and see what the commotion is all about."

The Fight:

Back on the highway, Sharon, now armed with a wheel brace, marched around to the back of the ambulance, flung open the back doors, frantically removed the two stretchers from the vehicle and hunted down the slithering creature.

Racing back and forth between the front cabin and the back compartment of the ambulance, Sharon kept up the fight delivering several blows to the reptile, who was undoubtedly just as frightened as she was.

Trying to escape the ferocious attacks from Sharon, the snake tried to escape through the back compartment, only to find it couldn't get a good grip on the well-polished floor.

At this stage, a motorist in a 4WD was approaching the ambulance from behind. As his eyes followed the long skid marks left on the road by the ambulance, he could see Sharon standing in the back compartment of the ambulance, delivering several strong blows with the wheel brace to the floor. Pulling over behind the ambulance, the man hopped out of his car and enquired as to whether she needed some help. With Sharon yelling that there was a snake, he quickly pulled open the front passenger door of the ambulance where, to the relief of the snake, it flew out past him and escaped into the bushes, all but a little bruised and exhausted from its ordeal.

Just at that moment the 'Cavaliers' arrived. The officer in charge, who laughingly admitted that he didn't like snakes, bravely wound the window down and from his seat called out to Sharon, "Are you all right?"

"Is the snake still around?" laughed Glen.

"Are you sure it was a snake?" continued the officer in charge.

Now that their 'knight in shining armour' image was tarnished, Sharon exclaimed,

"That's the last time I'll ask you to save me in my hour of need from venomous creatures!"

Stepping out of the vehicle, both the officer in charge and Glen helped Sharon tidy up and replace the stretchers back in the car. As Glen walked around the front of the ambulance, he bent down to pick up a stick. Using the stick, he then picked up something else from the table drain.

Approaching Sharon with the stick in his hand and a pair of ladies' underwear hanging off the end of the stick, he said, "Well, I see you've already changed your undies then."

27

Cat-astrophic

On a routine transport, Alan and his partner were taking a visually-impaired man to his doctor's appointment.

As they were wheeling the patient on the stretcher down the path at the front of the man's house, Alan could see a cat sprawled out in the middle of the path busily grooming itself.

As neither of the paramedics were great lovers of cats, Alan thought of a few ways to 'remove' it from the path. The idea of kicking the cat off the path would have given him a great deal of satisfaction, but realized this wouldn't be the ethical thing to do.

As they continued down the path and were getting closer to the cat, Alan was starting to think what an arrogant cat it was, because it continued lying on the path with no intention of moving out of their way.

In the meantime, Alan's partner was walking backwards at the other end of the stretcher and hadn't seen the cat. Before Alan could warn him that the cat was on the path, there was a loud screech followed by what sounded like a cat fight taking place under the stretcher.

As Alan looked under the stretcher to see what had happened, the nice placid cat that had been sunning itself on the path, had now turned into a deranged feline which resembled Animal from the television show *The Muppets*.

With its fur standing on end, ears flattened, mouth open, snarling, hissing and two round eyes giving that killer look, one very angry kitty was frantically clawing, kicking and biting at the stretcher wheel where its paw had become wedged.

In an attempt to remove itself from the obviously painful situation it was in, the cat continued to attack the wheel in an effort to break free. The dreadful sounds that emanated from under the stretcher had now alarmed the patient who was now becoming concerned about the welfare of his cat.

"What's wrong with my cat?"

"Er, um, just a slight accident," answered Alan. "We ran over your cat's paw with the stretcher."

"Why'd you do that for?" asked the patient.

"The cat wouldn't get out of the way and its paw got caught," replied Alan's partner.

"It's not the cat's fault it wouldn't get out of the way," retorted the patient. "He can't help it if he's blind!"

Penney Lang

Radio Talk

Paramedics In Stitches

28

Classic Comments

Dispatcher - "Proceed to (address). Patient unable to be woken. I think the patient is *currently* deceased."

****

Dispatcher - "Proceed to 'such and such' park to a hanging."

Paramedic - "Could you give us further directions to the location in the park?"

Dispatcher - "Oh, there should be someone hanging around who will direct you."

****

Paramedic - "I have a patient with a fractured humerus on the left leg."
(The humerus is the bone in the upper arm).

****

As the crew arrived at the scene of a truck rollover late one afternoon, we heard on the radio:

Paramedic - "Dispatch, we're arriving on-scene. This doesn't look good at all, I'll get back to you as soon as I can."

One minute later ...

"It's okay dispatch, it's only pasta sauce strewn all over the road."

****

While retrieving a thermometer from the response kit with his back to the patient.
Paramedic - "Okay mate, I'm gunna take yer temperature in yer ear."
On turning around to the patient he came face to face with the patient's backside.
"No, No. Not your rear, your ear mate, ear!" exclaimed the paramedic, while pointing to his own ear.

****

Dispatcher - "You're going to a two-month-old baby— not breathing, but is now crying."
(If the child is crying, then it must be capable of breathing).

****

Paramedic - "Dispatch, we've just been assaulted by our patient. He doesn't want to go to hospital, and he's just attacked us with his walking stick."

****

Dispatcher - "You're going to a patient who appears to have been unconscious at some stage during the night."

****

Conversation overheard between new student paramedic attending first block of training, and training officer during a scenario:

Training Officer - "Okay, so what are you going to do next?"

Student - "Ummm, Oh I know, call Triple Zero."

Training Officer - "Mate, you **ARE** Triple Zero!"

****

29

Ass No Questions

It is not often you find the communications staff stuck for words. Some paramedics also have the ability to completely stump the words of others on air … and get away with it.

This event occurred late one evening when an officer from another station called on the radio.

"Dispatch, there is a donkey wandering along the major road. Would you please notify the authorities to have it removed before someone has an accident."

Without blinking an eye, my partner Don suddenly reached for the radio mic. Pressing the microphone button, he asked, "Who left the Communications Centre door open?"

Later in the evening, the communications staff were asked why they didn't answer back.

"We couldn't," replied one officer.

"We just about fell off our chairs because we were laughing so much," explained another.

30

Fawlty Radios

There was a time when Ambulance Services didn't have the reliable radios we have today. Instead, the two-way radios were of the valve type which, unfortunately drew heaps of current, resulting in a flat battery in the vehicle within two to three hours if the radio was left on. Therefore, it became protocol that once the vehicle was parked, the radio must be switched off.

It was also customary for crews in the vicinity of the District Ambulance Centre to have morning tea at that station while waiting for patients to attend their routine appointments.

This was the case with a crew from an outlying station who, after dropping their patients off at their respective appointments, arrived at the District Ambulance Centre and turned off their car radio.

After finishing their morning break, the crew proceeded back to their station empty as their patients were not ready for return at this stage.

On the outskirts of the city, the officers realized that they hadn't turned the radio back on. Just as they did, the radio crackled to life and they heard their car number being called by dispatch. Turning to each other they realized they would be in all sorts of trouble for not having their radio on. So they answered dispatch back in a way that resembled the message being broken, with lots of background noise, indicating that there was something wrong with the radio.

As soon as the paramedics were back at their station, the dispatching officer was on the phone to them, blasting them for not answering the radio when called. The crew could only go along with what they had started, so they told the dispatcher, "The radio must be faulty because we did have it on."

"Well you could be right," replied the dispatcher. "I must admit, I couldn't quite understand your message."

"What would you like us to do then?" asked the paramedic in his most innocent voice.

"Sorry, but you'll need to drive back into the city and go to the radio technician's workshop," instructed the dispatcher.

Half an hour later, the technician still couldn't find any fault with the radio. Consequently a new radio was installed … one of the new solid-state type.

"This should solve your radio problems," smiled the technician.

Looking rather sheepish, the officers thanked the technician for his help.

Realizing the technician probably guessed what the real problem was, the paramedics quickly got back into the car before anything else was mentioned and headed back to the station.

The bonus was, of course, that the vehicle ended up with a brand new radio and the old valve set was retired (hopefully to a museum).

31

Malfunctioning Mic

After transporting a patient to the city hospital and returning back to an outlying station, the officer was curious as to where a persistent clicking sound was coming from.

All the way from the city the clicking sound continued and was about to drive him to distraction, when suddenly it stopped. Satisfied now that the problem had obviously rectified itself, he had a quieter trip for the remainder of his journey.

It wasn't until he arrived back at the station and went to notify the Communications Centre of this, that he found the radio cord was caught up in the car door. On opening the door, he saw the radio cord quickly retract back into the vehicle—minus the mouthpiece, which was now somewhere between the city and the ambulance station.

32

It Pays to be Honest

At times though, as most paramedics would agree, it does become annoying that one must inform the communications officers of every move, even if they slightly divert their course while on their way back to the station.

It was therefore common practice that when an officer needed to go somewhere out of his designated area, the officer would request a routine case in the vicinity of where he needed to conduct his business, therefore having an excuse for being in that particular area. Doing this saved a lot of paperwork, as the following account shows.

Informing the communications staff that he was clear from the city hospital, a certain officer was directed to return to the District Ambulance Centre for morning tea. After not hearing from this officer for some time, the senior communications officer concluded that the paramedic must have picked up some morning tea for himself on the way.

Shortly afterwards, a phone call was received from that officer informing the communications centre that he had been involved in an accident.

Initially the emergency call taker thought the paramedic was joking. After much convincing, he explained that both he and the occupants of the other vehicle were all right.

The problem was, however, that the officer was nowhere near where he should have been, but was in another suburb … on the other side of the city.

Consequently, the dispatching officer didn't have any notes on the job card that the officer was doing a 'foreigner' on the southside.

This resulted in the officer spending the rest of his shift writing reports; not only on the accident, which extensively damaged the other vehicle, but also explaining why he wasn't in the area that he was directed to.

33

The Numbers Game

A variety of codes are used in the Emergency Services and other departments in relation to specific tasks. It may be the response code of vehicles on a job, or a discreet message to the emergency call taker indicating that an officer is in trouble and needs police assistance urgently. This is fine, as long as the person at the receiving end is able to decipher the code.

On returning to the station late one evening from the hospital, we came to a set of traffic lights. Mark, who was driving, slowed down and stopped at the lights. His partner turned to him and asked, "Why have we stopped? The lights are green."

"Yeah I know," replied Mark. "But we've been going through the red ones all night, so I figured we would stop at the green ones instead." Continuing on Mark asked, "How 'bout a 4-1-1?"

"Sounds like a good idea," replied his partner.

Mark picked up the mic and called the Communications Centre.

"Dispatch, this is unit 517, requesting a 4-1-1 at 711 and then a 4-1-2 at 1-8-5 and at the same time indulge in a 4-1-3 please."

Silence for a good ten seconds and then finally a very slow, "Rrroggerrr?"

This is basically translated as: "Dispatch this is Unit 517, requesting a meal pick-up at 711 (store name) and then we'll proceed to the station for a sustenance break and eat dinner."

We're not sure even to this day whether the dispatcher actually understood the message.

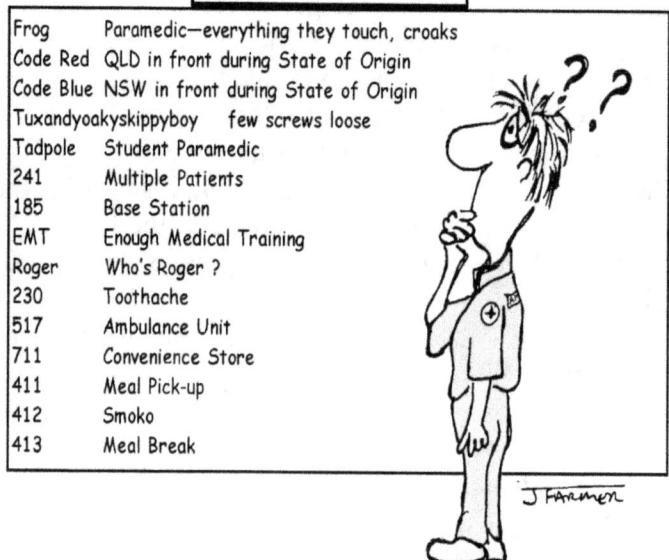

COMMS CODES

Frog	Paramedic—everything they touch, croaks
Code Red	QLD in front during State of Origin
Code Blue	NSW in front during State of Origin
Tuxandyoakyskippyboy	few screws loose
Tadpole	Student Paramedic
241	Multiple Patients
185	Base Station
EMT	Enough Medical Training
Roger	Who's Roger ?
230	Toothache
517	Ambulance Unit
711	Convenience Store
411	Meal Pick-up
412	Smoko
413	Meal Break

J FARMER

34

Wake-up Call

If you have ever had the opportunity to ride in the front of an ambulance, have you wondered why the number of the ambulance unit is displayed at various places in the front cab, such as on the microphone or on the dash?

In towns outside of the metropolitan areas, paramedics are often on-call or on emergency availability, after having completed either an eight or ten hour shift. Apart from their normal day shift, they are required to respond immediately to any cases that come in at all hours of the night.

Being woken from a deep sleep in the early hours of the morning has its disadvantages, especially for those who love the comfort of their nice warm bed. Giving it up on a cold winter morning is extremely difficult.

However, if you find you have an energetic paramedic at two in the morning, you've either got a brand new student or a paramedic who's just had caffeine intravenously.

For some of us, though, waking up to find the phone ringing, and then knowing you are expected to respond straight away, can be a real test. To have the alertness of someone who has been awake already for a few hours (and has consumed coffee), can be a difficult task, as some things don't seem to work as well as they should. This includes co-ordination between the brain and the mouth. Sometimes the two will not connect straight away and consequently communicating with others can be a challenge.

This was the plight of a paramedic who responded to a case during the early hours of one morning, where she was to meet her partner on-scene. On arriving, she notified the communications centre that she was on-scene with these words:

"Dispatch, this is unit 422 … aahh 210 ... umm No! 320 ... uhhh 3 … oh hell, I don't know which car I'm in now, but I'm on-scene!"

Consequently, when her partner arrived, he had to notify dispatch which units were actually on-scene.

35

Piggy Questions

During the H1N1 influenza pandemic (known as swine flu), emergency medical dispatch officers were required to ask callers additional questions in relation to the swine flu. This was so that the paramedics could take safety precautions if there was any indication that the patient may have contracted the virus.

After having a banter with fellow emergency call takers, referring to the swine flu as 'piggy flu', a certain emergency call taker then took a call from a patient whose symptoms indicated that further information was required regarding the H1N1 virus.

The emergency call taker was overheard saying to the caller, "Now I just need to ask you some piggy questions, er, I mean, some questions regarding the swine flu."

Paramedics In Stitches

Practical Jokes

Paramedics In Stitches

36

Toeing the Line

Some paramedics have the ability to get away with things most people would not dare mention. Such is the case with an officer named Dave.

Due to the growing number of requests for clinical transports, the Ambulance Service introduced the Patient Transport Service. This team of dedicated officers is responsible for transporting hundreds of people every day to and from various medical appointments with the same care and dedication as their paramedic colleagues.

Before the Patient Transport Service was introduced, ambulance officers were rostered on at certain times during the rotation to conduct this service. In many cases, there was only one officer assigned to the clinic bus, as there was no need for any clinical intervention for the patient.

One ambulance station used a HiAce van for these clinical transports, which usually had one stretcher and a couple of seats. Due to the Workplace Health and Safety Regulation, wheelchairs and walkers were not allowed in the vehicle with the patient as there was no way of stowing them safely.

One day, Dave was rostered on the clinic bus and was required to transport a 72-year-old female for a specialist appointment at the hospital.

Arriving at the patient's residence, he found it was an old highset house. At the top of the stairs he was met by a lady sitting in a wheelchair surrounded by her family. Due to complications with diabetes, the lady was now a double leg amputee and demanded that she take her wheelchair with her.

Dave tactfully tried to explain to her that there was no way he could take the wheelchair as it would become a projectile in the back of the ambulance if he had an accident. However the patient became more and more insistent that the wheelchair should go with her.

At this Dave said, "Look, the only way we can do this is to tow the wheelchair behind the ambulance."

"Yep, that's fine," replied the patient.

Dave raised his eyebrows on hearing this. He then looked at the family members and was surprised to see the patient's family nodding in agreement.

"All right then," he said in disbelief.

With that, he requested the family to carry the wheelchair down the stairs and place it at the back of the ambulance. Meanwhile he cradled the lady in his arms, carried her downstairs, and sat her back in the wheelchair.

Standing back, Dave now instructed her: "Because you are the owner/operator of this wheelchair, by law, you are required to operate this vehicle behind the ambulance while I'm towing you."

The lady now hesitated saying, "I don't know about this."

Meanwhile, the lady's family was grinning and giggling away, thinking that Dave was playing a joke on her.

As Dave grabbed some jumper leads from the ambulance, he continued on ...

"Okay, so this is what we're going to do. I'm going to connect you up with these jumper leads, 'cause that's all I've got to attach the wheelchair to the ambulance with."

Dave proceeded to clip the leads to either side of the rear bullbar on the ambulance. He then attached the other ends of the leads to both handrails of the wheelchair.

"Now listen closely," he added. "There are road rules that we have to abide by. So when I put my left indicator on, you need to pull on the left jumper lead so that the wheelchair will travel around to the left. When I go to the right, you pull on the right lead. Then, when you see the brake lights come on, I want you to pull on both leads together and yell out in a loud voice, 'Whhoooo' so that I know you understand that I'm braking, and you aren't going to run up the back of the ambulance."

After pausing for a bit to allow the information to sink in, Dave asked the lady, "So are you right with that?"

"Yes, yes I understand."

"Okay then, we'll have a practise run first, just to make sure everything's good."

While Dave moved to the driver's compartment, the lady grabbed hold of the leads, one in each hand, ready to go.

Standing beside the driver's door, Dave reached inside and activated the left indicator, prompting the lady to pull on the left jumper lead. Dave called out, "Did you get that?"

"Yes," came the reply as she continued to tug on the lead.

Repeating the action with the right indicator, Dave called out again, "Have you got that?"

"Yes," she called out and pulled on the right jumper lead.

"Okay, good. Now hang on and I'll just push on the brake."

As he pushed on the brake, he heard the lady yell out, "Whhoooo," and saw her pulling on both jumper leads like she was pulling up a horse.

Walking back to the lady, Dave asked her, "Now, are you sure you're ready to go?"

With beads of sweat forming on her brow, she tightened her grip on the leads firmly and anxiously replied, "Yes, yes, I think so."

As Dave hopped in the driver's seat and turned the ignition, the lady's family suddenly started waving their arms about and yelling, "Whooah, whooah! What are you doing? What are you doing?"

Dave leaned out the window and yelled back to them, "What. What's wrong? This is the way it's done!"

"No. No. You can't do that!" they cried.

After turning off the ignition, Dave jumped out of the ambulance and walked up to the family saying, "Well, you guys are just going to have to take the wheelchair instead then."

In a serious and relieved voice they nodded their heads frantically saying, "Oh yeah, we'll take the wheelchair mate, no worries mate."

So Dave loaded the patient onto the stretcher, as he had intended to do in the first place, and proceeded to transport the lady in time for her appointment.

37

Microwave Biscuits

When microwave ovens were introduced into households, ambulance stations around the state also took advantage of the new invention. It was great to be able to reheat your meal after having to desert it suddenly to attend to a case.

One of the ambulance officers called Bob, told the administration girl that he had brought in some 'microwave bickies'.

"Go on try them," he urged her.

She took one of the little round 'bickies', which looked like a miniature doughnut and popped it into her mouth.

Biting down on it, she found it was a bit hard to chew. As her taste buds tried to decipher this strange new sensation, she almost immediately spat the biscuit out saying that it tasted terrible and wouldn't have any more.

At that moment she knew she had been set up ... especially when the other staff members in the room burst out laughing. They informed her that Bob's microwave bickies were actually dog biscuits.

Consequently, for about a week afterwards, she was referred to as 'Lassie'.

38

Town Crier

Children translate the sound of a siren into the English language as: *eeeee aww eeeee aww*, or *rrrrr rr rrrrr rr*. Adults change the translation to: *It's meeeee mum, it's meeeee mum, it's meeeee mum*. (I'm sure you have some creations of your own).

People who have never been in an ambulance before find all the buttons and dials fascinating, and so the inevitable questions are asked:

"Which one's the siren?"

"Can I turn it on?"

My partner Julie and I were transporting two overseas tourists. The patient, who was quite stable, was in the back with Julie treating; her travelling companion was seated beside me in the passenger's seat.

For the bored paramedic, overseas tourists can be fun. Here they are in an unfamiliar country, where rules and regulations are different from what they are accustomed to. To make it even more difficult, they have no idea of the great Aussie sense of humour and may be easily mislead. (All in the name of broadening one's horizons I believe).

On the way to the hospital, I could see the male tourist carefully examining the panel of buttons and dials. It would be safe to say that I was feeling a tad mischievous at this particular moment. Finally he asked the question I had been waiting for:

"Which one is the siren?"

"Unfortunately this is an old ambulance and the siren that came with it doesn't work any more," I replied.

"So what do you do then, if you have an emergency and you need to make the traffic move out of the way?" he asked, somewhat confused.

"See that bullbar at the front of the ambulance?"

"Yes," he nodded.

"Well, when we are on an emergency call, Julie, who is currently in the back, sits on the bullbar. As we race through the streets she calls out, 'Scuuuse me, scuuuse me, scuuuse me,' as loud as she can."

A screech of laughter suddenly erupted from Julie in the back. That was the end of her. She couldn't stop laughing until we arrived at the hospital.

Meanwhile my male tourist was left a little confused at first and for a moment wasn't sure whether or not to laugh.

39

Goldilocks

A mental health facility, which was situated near an ambulance station, had twelve wards, each of which was used for a different purpose. Wards 11 and 12 were classed as lockdown units, where the more severe cases were kept.

The ambulance station had been built fairly close to Ward 12.

Many stations in the area worked the same roster. Over a seven-week period, the crews of all stations working on line one, would be the same crews working the following week on line two and so on.

Back-filling of stations would often happen. For example, a crew from station (A) would be required to cover station (B) when the crew from station (B) happened to be working in another area. Therefore an interchange of officers and stations would take place.

This resulted in a group of people meeting up on a regular basis, and so a rapport was built between the officers of various stations working the same shift. Sometimes they would assist each other on cases, but these instances weren't the only times where teamwork was essential.

One particular crew, consisting of Tom and his partner, were on night shift. As it turned out, it was a busy night with the crew hardly stepping foot inside the door of their home station. They had been standing by at another station on and off for most of the evening. Therefore, the crew from another nearby station (one of whom was a great practical joker), had been sent to backfill Tom's station.

At one stage during the evening, as Tom and his partner were returning from the hospital, the emergency medical dispatcher informed the crew—over the radio airwaves—they had just been notified by the mental health facility that a female patient had escaped from Ward 12. The dispatcher further described the patient as slightly built with short blonde hair. He warned them that she was a known nymphomaniac and not to approach the patient if they did see her, as her medical condition was unstable and she might become violent.

As the night progressed with many calls keeping the paramedics busy, the dispatching officers reminded the crew several times over the air—which the whole region heard—of the female escapee, and not to approach her. They also requested that the crew check the station for any signs that the patient could be hiding inside the station. However, due to the workload, the crew never got back to the station long enough to check for the whereabouts of the female patient.

It wasn't until about three in the morning that the crew finally returned to their home station. Tom informed his partner that he was exhausted and was going to lay down for awhile.

Walking into the bedroom and not bothering to turn on the light, Tom started to take off his boots. As he approached the bed, he could see what appeared to be a blonde female, fitting the description of the escaped patient, asleep under the bed covers.

Tom quickly crept out of the bedroom to alert his partner.

"Mate, this girl is in my bedroom," whispered Tom.

"You've got to be joking," replied his partner.

"No, I'm not!" exclaimed Tom.

Tiptoeing up to the bedroom, Tom's partner then poked his head around the door and whispered back to him, "You're right! That looks like her."

So they snuck out to the ambulance, started the car up and activated the large roller doors to the station, ready for a hasty exodus.

Tom then called on the radio to the communications centre and announced, "Dispatch, that female who has escaped from the mental health facility is actually asleep in one of the beds at our station. You'll need to contact the police and get them down here ASAP!"

The only response they got from the dispatching officer was an hysterical laugh, followed by, "Gotcha!" from another crew.

The joke was well and truly on Tom. The majority of the region's crews, including the communications centre staff, were all 'in the know'. Tom's partner who was also in on it, did an excellent job of playing along with it right from the start.

So, who was in Tom's bed …

Arriving back at the station, Tom went into the bedroom and turned on the light to find 'Resusci Anne', the training mannequin, looking quite comfortable in his bed.

40

Anybody for Takeaway?

It amuses me that at times when an ambulance pulls up somewhere, people often assume there is a patient in the back—even when you buy food at the drive-through of a takeaway store. (Surprisingly, paramedics have to eat also).

Inevitably the day came when I was ordering a meal and the young girl on the other side of the drive-through window leaned out and asked me, "Do you have anybody in the back?"

"Yes," I replied.

"Really?" she said in a surprised tone

"But the patient died," I whispered back to her.

"You mean there's a body in the back?" she gasped in horror.

"Yep," I replied. "So we don't need to order anything for him now."

It wasn't until she came back with our meals that she realized we weren't serious.

Another opportunity came when I was refuelling the ambulance at the local fuel depot, when a man pulled up in his 4WD vehicle.

As he had to wait until I had finished refuelling, the usual greetings and small talk ensued. Eventually he turned to me and asked, "Do you have anybody in the back?"

"Yes, but they died," I replied in a serious tone.

"Oh," was his shocked reply.

After some silence, he then asked, "Male or female?"

I thought for a moment, then replied, "It doesn't really matter now does it?"

"No, I guess not," he surmised.

The gentleman and I chatted on a bit more, before he finally stated, "I think you're pulling my leg, aren't you?"

With a big grin, I finished refuelling and then turned to him nodding, "Yes, I'm afraid I am."

We both had a laugh and then I walked off to pay for the fuel.

41

Fish Food

The lengths some people go to in order to carry out a practical joke is unbelievable. Before embarking on their career as paramedics, some officers were tradesmen.

A well-known practical joker came into work one day, ready to play a joke on one of his colleagues. A few days previously, he'd surreptitiously taken measurements, obtained some glass, silicon glue and everything else required for 'the project'.

Removing the contents from his colleague's food locker, he carefully glued up any holes or cracks within the locker. Taking a sheet of glass, he stood the glass panel up so that it fitted neatly into the front of the locker, allowing enough room for the door to close properly. He also made sure that there was approximately a ten-centimetre gap between the edge of the glass and the ceiling of the locker.

Gravel and water were then poured into the improvised fish tank, along with some little ornaments and other bits and pieces to set it off nicely. Finally, a few fish were added!

One can only imagine the surprise and look on his colleague's face, when he returned to work and opened his food locker to find some fish swimming around where his own food should have been.

42

Just Hangin' with the Gang

Over the years, various pieces of equipment have been introduced into the Ambulance Service, allowing officers to extricate patients safely from dangerous situations. One particular piece of equipment was the Paraguard Stretcher, a rescue stretcher designed for use in mine rescues. The stretcher, when folded in half, turned into a type of backpack. This enabled the rescuer to strap it to his back, making it easier to carry into the mine shaft. Once unfolded, the device had flaps which were tied around the patient's chest, abdomen, hips and legs. It also contained carry handles and points where the apparatus could be attached to a winch, so that the patient could be removed from the mine by a helicopter.

Many years later, a new device was introduced. This was called the Kendrick Extrication Device, otherwise known as the KED. It enabled officers to safely remove patients with suspected spinal injuries from a smashed-up vehicle.

This looked similar to the Paraguard Stretcher and was placed down along the patient's back. It supported the head and the spine down to the lower back. The KED, used in conjunction with a cervical collar, was secured with a series of straps around the patient's head, chest, abdomen and thighs.

Now securely wrapped up in the KED (that resembled a full body corset) the patient was unable to move their head or twist their back as they were being extricated from the vehicle.

On a particularly slow morning, a number of officers decided to take advantage of the downtime to practise using the new KED. Joan, who was in her sixties, worked in the office as the administration assistant. She was always a good target for a bit of practise and was often used as a 'patient' due to her small stature and light weight. Once again she was coaxed from the office to assist the boys in some training. Sitting comfortably on a chair, the officers proceeded to strap Joan up in the KED.

With Joan now trussed up and confident that she couldn't go anywhere, the officers realized that it was now morning tea time. Satisfied that the KED had been firmly applied, they picked Joan up and carried her outside to where the flagpole was situated at the front of the ambulance station. However, after assessing the situation, they decided Joan may be a little too heavy for the flagpole lanyard, so they hoisted a pair of boxer shorts up there instead. The paramedics then carried Joan into the plant room (where the ambulances are parked), and proceeded to hang her on a hook up on the wall.

With Joan's arms and legs flailing helplessly, and her feeble cries for help falling on deaf ears, the boys walked off leaving her hanging on the wall in full view of the passing traffic on the nearby main road.

Wondering what the commotion was all about,

the officer in charge stuck his head around the door to see poor Joan hooked up on the wall. After having a little chuckle to himself, he decided he'd better come to her rescue or he wouldn't get any of his office work done at all.

In the meantime, those boxer shorts fluttered about on the flagpole for a good twenty-four hours before anybody noticed.

43

Handle with Care

It was approximately eleven thirty at night when two crews were called to a male patient with traumatic injuries to his arm. They were directed about 300 metres from the railway station down the railway track to where the patient was lying on the ground. One of his friends was holding a pullover firmly against the patient's forearm, in the place where his hand should have been.

The group of youths had decided to take a shortcut. They were walking close to the railway tracks when, suddenly, a train came around the corner hitting the male youth.

As three of the paramedics transported the patient to hospital, George stayed back to look for the missing appendage. As the ambulance departed with the patient, two police officers arrived on the scene and approached George.

It was pitch-black and, without the moon, finding the missing hand was going to be a bit difficult. So George asked the two police officers if they would help. Turning to them George asked, "Have either of you ever been to a train incident like this?"

"No," both of them replied.

George said, "Well, you'll need to be careful, because dealing with an amputated hand can be especially tricky. The nerves are usually still twitching and it can sometimes grab you quite suddenly if you're not aware of this," he stated in all seriousness.

"Oh rubbish!" replied the policewoman. "That doesn't happen."

"Oh, yes it does!" George continued. "Just like a chook with its head cut off still twitches and carries on, so does an amputated hand."

With that, he turned and headed for the remaining ambulance calling out over his shoulder, "I'm just going to get a couple of torches for us."

"Well, hurry back then 'cause I'm feeling a bit nervous with that hand lying about," the policewoman joked.

Grabbing a couple of torches from the ambulance, George started to make his way back to where the police officers were standing. With no other lights to light up the area, George reverted to his military days of ambush tactics. He crouched down low in the darkness and listened for any movement which would guide him back to the police officers. Suddenly, one lit up a cigarette. George crept a bit closer trying not to make a sound. He could hear the murmur of their voices followed by, "Shhh, did you hear that?"

"What was it?" asked the other.

George stopped in his tracks, frozen.

"Nothing, I just thought I heard a noise."

The officer drew on the cigarette again, alerting George that he was very close to them.

Just one step closer, he thought to himself.

Then he heard the policewoman ask, "Where's that paramedic and those torches? I can't see a thing here."

"You're not scared are you?" her partner asked. "You sound a bit tense."

"I just hate being in the dark, that's all!"

Holding out his hand, George stretched his fingers as far as they would go. Nothing! With his heart thumping against his chest, he inched closer. Suddenly he felt the material of the police officer's trouser leg. Stiffening his hand, he suddenly lunged his hand forward and grabbed onto the ankle.

The policewoman let out an almighty scream. "Ahhh, ahhh! It's got me, It's got me. Get it off!" she bellowed. At the same time she pulled her gun from the holster.

George couldn't contain himself any longer and rolled around on the ground laughing hysterically.

"I nearly shot you!" exclaimed the policewoman as she playfully kicked George in the ribs while calling him all the names under the sun.

Once everybody had regained their composure, they continued on with the search by torchlight. Shortly thereafter they found the appendage and arranged for it to be transported to the hospital where its owner had been taken.

44

Don't let the Bedbugs Bite

A certain control officer was said to be absolutely petrified of snakes. One night when he was on a late shift, one of the officers slipped a rubber snake under the covers of his nicely made up bed.

At one o'clock in the morning, when all was quiet, the control officer decided to take a nap. Stripping down to his underwear, he walked over to the bed, pulled back the sheets and revealed the curled up 'reptile' lying in the middle of his bed.

Having just received the fright of his life, he let out a bellow and leapt through the open window of the bedroom, into the warm summer night. (Thank goodness it was a lowset building.)

Locking the window behind him, his fellow officers were in fits of laughter. They watched through the window as a near-naked control officer ran around the ambulance grounds in his underwear.

He brought more attention to himself by making a racket, as he looked for a way to get back inside. Banging on the locked doors and windows, he continued yelling at the top of his voice to the officers who were too busy laughing to let him in.

45

Long Way Home

Having transported this particular male patient on a regular basis over several years, Steve had developed a good rapport with him. The man was a war veteran who had both legs amputated many years ago and Steve was about to return him home in the clinic ambulance following a specialist appointment at the hospital.

Parking the wheelchair next to the driver's door, Steve said, "Look, I've had a really rough day and I'm sick of driving, so I'm going to get you to drive."

He then opened the driver's door, lifted the patient from the wheelchair and sat him in the driver's seat. Before the patient could say anything, Steve closed the driver's door and scooted around the front of the ambulance to the passenger side.

On settling himself into the passenger's seat, the patient turned to Steve and protested,

"But I can't drive this!"

"Of course you can," Steve said.

"No, I really can't drive," replied the patient becoming anxious.

"You've got a licence haven't you?" inquired Steve.

"No, but that's not the reason."

"Well what's wrong then?" asked Steve.

140

The patient leaned over toward Steve and whispered, "I haven't got any legs."
In mock disbelief, Steve sat back staring at the man.

"You are joking, right?"

"No!" replied the patient pointing to his stumps. "See!"

Rolling his eyes Steve let out an exasperated, "Oh, all right. Slide across and I'll do the driving then."

Steve then lowered the handbrake, assisted his 'co-pilot' to slide across into the passenger's seat and proceeded to drive him home.

Paramedics In Stitches

Penney Lang

Lessons
Learned

Paramedics In Stitches

46

A Duck in Time

When rostered on the clinic run, officers would have the time to get to know the patients they were regularly transporting.

One elderly lady, whose eyesight was failing, was transported on a regular basis and often sat in the front seat of the ambulance. Unfortunately she was infamously known for her negative and condescending comments, targeting the people she knew at the nursing home where she lived. Nothing would stop this woman from her slanderous remarks. The poor officer transporting her had to endure this continual gossip throughout the entire journey.

Unable to withstand one more minute of this woman's nagging, one officer, quite by mistake, came up with an unusual solution. He passed on this newfound knowledge to other officers who had unfortunately drawn the 'short straw'.

The Solution:

As the ambulance drove down a particular road, which was lined with light poles, the officers made sure they would drive as close to the gutter as possible. With each light pole they approached, the old lady would suddenly duck her head to 'miss' the light pole. She was obviously frightened that the ambulance was about to 'clean up' each pole they were heading for. This worked so well that as she concentrated more on missing the light poles, she soon forgot about her nagging.

You could say 'the old nag' became 'the old duck'.

47

Mr Snuggles

There was a time when it was common practice for ambulance officers to have a second job. Therefore you could do a night shift, sleep most of the night, and turn up for your day job the next day.

Most crews adhered to the night shift policy that you were not to go to bed before 11 p.m. and you had to be up before 6 a.m. One crew, however, thought they were an exception.

The officer in charge would always find this crew still sound asleep when he arrived for work the next morning at 6.45. Despite speaking to them several times about the night shift policy, and the fact they were expected to comply like everybody else, this crew continued to ignore his warnings until, finally, his patience ran out.

On arriving at work one morning at 6.40 when this crew were on, he found the station quiet, except for the sound of snoring coming from the bedroom. As quiet as a mouse, he crept into the bedroom and found Phil, who was the senior officer, fast asleep.

Taking off his boots, he gently sat on the edge of the bed and then laid down next to Phil. Putting his arm around him, he whispered in his ear, "I'm so glad you're still in bed, Phillip."

Phil flew out of bed so fast that his feet didn't touch the floor until he was halfway out the door.

The officer in charge never had a problem again with the crews sleeping in of a morning.

48

Fell off the Back of a Truck

Pulling up at a set of traffic lights while doing a routine transport, I noticed that the truck in front of me, in the next lane, was laden with boxes of alcohol. The saying, 'fell off the back of a truck,' quickly entered my mind and I was just thinking how easy it would be for someone to steal some of the alcohol as none of it was covered and the truck's tray had no sides.

I looked at the car in front of me and, sure enough, the passenger door opened and out jumped a young male who proceeded to run up to the back of the truck. As the young man helped himself to a carton of Jim Beam, I felt I had to do something to prevent the theft but couldn't just jump out of the ambulance and chase him. Instead, I pressed my hand on the car horn making as much noise as possible. Suddenly, other vehicles around me also started to sound their car horns.

The racket caused the young thief to panic and as he started to run down the footpath he lost his footing. Unable to stop himself from tripping over, he dropped the carton of alcohol and ended up sprawled across the ground. Unfortunately, he managed to run off with two bottles, but at least the truck driver was made aware of the situation and retrieved the rest of the stolen goods.

49

Sweet Revenge

When women started joining the ranks of the Ambulance Service, some male officers were not so keen on the idea. While some were outright nasty and taunted my female colleagues for many years, most men took it in their stride and accepted that this was a positive step for the Ambulance Service.

Officers at one particular station found themselves in this situation when Tanya became the first full-time female ambulance officer at their station.

Not long after the introductions and a quick tour of the ambulance station, the new recruit found herself proceeding on her first emergency call. Proving to the senior officers that their new officer could pull her weight, Tanya did her best in each situation she was faced with. It wasn't long before Tanya earned the respect of her older male colleagues and was eventually treated as 'one of the guys'.

Although 'the boys' were quite protective of Tanya, this didn't stop them from playing the odd practical joke on her, especially when she was on night shift. These jokes included short-sheeting her bed or stitching up the arm and leg holes of her overalls, which had been laid out neatly in readiness for a late night or early morning call. Subsequent female officers who started work at this station were often 'scared to death' by a frozen dead snake that landed on the newspaper they were trying to read.

Before the Fire or Police Services took on the role of using the jaws-of-life to cut people out of smashed-up vehicles, ambulance officers were assigned this task. They were required to carry the cutting gear, and other equipment for such extrications, in ambulances or any other vehicles that were used specifically for road rescue.

While preparing some wood chocks (to prevent vehicles from rolling), a couple of male officers were having a bit of trouble using the saw to cut the wood.

They decided they needed something to grease the saw. They asked Tanya to go to the butcher and get a big bag of suet (hard white fat surrounding the kidneys of grazing animals). However, Tanya suspected that they might be playing a joke on her, so she asked the station officer if this request sounded right.

In a serious tone, he replied, "If that's what they've asked you do, then you'll have to do it."

Knowing that she was possibly being set up, Tanya proceeded down the road to the butcher. Maybe it was the grin on the butcher's face that gave it away, but she sensed the butcher might have received a phone call from a certain ambulance.

With a huge bag of suet in her hands, Tanya made her way back to the ambulance station where she formulated a cunning plan ...

The lamingtons looked perfect; neatly cut up into nice, bite-sized pieces and coated with a thin layer of chocolate and coconut. The suet lamingtons looked inviting, especially to some sweet-toothed male ambulance officers who were in need of a midnight snack while on night shift.

Only one took the bait. As her male colleague shoved the lamington into his mouth and attempted to bite into the lard, a burst of laughter came from his counterparts. Having swallowed half the lamington, he threw the remainder at Tanya, along with a barrage of derogatory comments.

50

Hazardous Materials

My husband and I were staying with a friend for a few days in a town where we used to work. While sleeping in the spare bedroom downstairs, we were woken early one morning to the sound of a smoke alarm going off.

The alarm was intermittent and muffled and, in our half asleep state, we wondered if the smoke alarm noise was coming from the house next door. To our relief, the noise stopped and we drifted back to sleep again.

Suddenly, the alarm started up again, only this time it was piercingly louder. We were now wide awake. Sitting up in bed, we said to each other that we couldn't smell smoke, however, we could hear a crackling sound coming from upstairs. Suddenly, we heard an almighty thump directly above us.

Diving out of bed, I ran to the doorway to find our friend racing down the stairs toward us.

"There's a small electrical fire in the kitchen!" she exclaimed. "The dishwasher is on fire!"

Racing upstairs we found the dishwasher in the middle of the kitchen on fire. We found out later that, without realizing what she was doing, the amount of adrenaline surging through our friend's bloodstream had given her the strength to pull the dishwasher out from the adjoining cupboards.

As we attempted to smother the fire, we soon realised that this wasn't going to work. So we ran back downstairs and outside to turn off the main power supply to the house. My husband and friend then grabbed the garden hose and raced up the back stairs. However, by this time there was a lot of smoke billowing out from the kitchen so they retreated downstairs and out onto the footpath to wait for the Fire Brigade that I had called in the meantime.

When the Fire Brigade arrived, it was only then we noticed my husband was just wearing his jocks. The fire officers wouldn't let him back inside, not even to retrieve his trousers, until they deemed it was safe for us.

It wasn't long before we heard another siren approaching and we turned around to see an ambulance pulling up. Jumping out of the ambulance was a former student I had previously mentored. Now qualified, he was obviously mentoring his partner who was a student. Like most keen students, this young man wanted to assess my husband and friend for any smoke inhalation.

Not realizing we were paramedics, the student raced over toward us with his stethoscope in hand. Intent on listening to my husband's chest, the student kept on trying to talk my husband into being assessed.

"It's all right mate, I'm okay," said my husband putting up his hands to stop the student.

"Just let me have a listen to make sure you're okay," the student protested.

Embarrassed to be caught standing on the footpath in his jocks, my husband didn't want anything to do with the student. Eventually, the paramedic told the student that we were also paramedics. After much discussion though, my husband finally agreed to let the student check him over to satisfy everyone that there wasn't anything wrong.

The following day, after we arrived back home, we immediately bought two fire extinguishers. Placing one in our bedroom and the other near the kitchen.

This frightening experience taught us a few lessons:

One: Always have a torch handy beside the bed. These days we never go away without packing a torch, and it always sits beside the bed.

Two: Always be kind to the junior officers because you never know when you'll be in an embarrassing situation and in need their help.

Three: Make sure you know where your trousers are at all times.

Penney Lang

Country
Characters

Paramedics In Stitches

51

Cheeky Challenge

It is not unusual for paramedics, police and fire officers to engage in a sporting challenge—service against service—at least once a year. In most areas, this might include a football or cricket match, but not so in one little town. They preferred to get down and play dirty, with a 'Buck-Off Emergency Services Challenge' held in conjunction with the annual rodeo.

Now you might think that riding a tonne of hamburger steak might not be your choice of fun—nor mine for that matter—but boys will be boys. As they put it: "It's all for a good cause!"

The event, which had run for six consecutive years, was a charity fundraiser for one of the local community groups. The Ambulance Service were the reigning champions so far with a total of three wins. Runners-up were the Police Service with two, and the Fire Service had won the trophy once a couple of years earlier.

Each year for six years, local paramedic Dan would replace his uniform with a cowboy hat, chaps and spurs, ready for the ride of his life! He was always nervous before his ride, but this year was special. Dan had heard that it might be the last year that the rodeo would be held. He really wanted to do his best and put the Ambulance Service in the spotlight by winning the trophy for a fourth time.

Straddled over the back of the huge beast called Thunder, Dan made sure his hand was securely fastened under the rope, which was his only means of hanging on.

As the boys made sure the bull's horns weren't caught up in the rails, Dan slowly settled on the back of the huge beast, and then called for the gate to be released.

As the gate swung wide open, out jumped the bull kicking his back legs from side to side in an attempt to dump the weight from his back. At the same time, Dan threw one hand in the air and stuck the spurs into the side of the beast whenever he got the chance. Meanwhile, gripping the rope with his other hand which was strapped to the beast, he hung on for dear life.

It was all over too soon. The bull had started to spin around, and its rear legs gave an almighty kick causing Dan to lose his grip. After being flung like a rag doll through the air, Dan fell to the earth, ploughing a trench into the dirt with his body until he finally came to rest.

The bull then turned to face the annoying object it had successfully thrown off. Dan looked up in time to see the bull heading for him. In a panic, he tried to scramble across the dusty ground. However, the bull's horns swiped at his backside before he could climb out of its reach, leaving him with a large tear in his jeans.

Suddenly, the rodeo clown appeared at Dan's side sheltering him from any further strikes the bull might make.

The announcer's voice now filled the air as Dan's time and score were read out. He'd just made the eight seconds. This would place him in the lead against his Emergency Services competitors.

Dan proudly threw his hat in the air, waving to the cheering crowd. As he turned and bent over to pick up his hat from the ground, the crowd suddenly burst into laughter amid a series of wolf whistles.

Confused as to what had drawn the crowd's attention, Dan climbed the rodeo arena's rails. As he flung his leg over the top rail, he felt a slight chill to his rear end. Looking over his right shoulder, he just caught a glimpse of white flesh poking out through the seat of his blue jeans. Then it dawned on him that he had just 'mooned' the entire town in which he lived.

That's one way of putting the Ambulance Service in the spotlight!

52

The Ride

This poem came about while I was attending a rodeo in December 2006, which was a fundraiser for the Royal Flying Doctor Service and the local ambulance.

I was watching two young lads who were dressed up in their cowboy shirts, hats and boots, standing ringside taking in all the action.

Imitating their fathers, they placed one little boot on the bottom rail. Leaning on the third rail, they watched in awe as men flew out of the chutes and attempted to ride on the backs of bulls and horses.

However, the big event that these boys were waiting for was the Poddy Ride (A poddy is a hand-reared calf). Like the Bull Ride event, the boys, and some girls, were required to stay on the poddy calf for eight seconds.

As the time drew closer for this event, they were excitedly acting out the movements in readiness for ... *The Ride.*

The Ride

Looking the part, he pulls on the chaps,
Over his boots, the spurs are all strapped;
A buckle so big, it shines in the sun,
He's gettin' excited, for this is the one.

He might be six, but feels like a man,
His foot on the rail, he thinks up a plan;
Got his cowboy hat, he wears it with pride,
He's gearin' up, for the great Poddy Ride.

His hands are sweaty, as he stands in line,
This time, he thinks, I'll take me time.
His heart is thumping, against his chest,
There with his mates are Steve and Mike West.

"Righto young fella, this is ya beast,
Hop right on, and take a seat."
With a clang of the gate, it opens wide,
Out flies the poddy, and kicks to each side.

It's all over too soon, as he falls in the sand,
His dad is beside him, to give him a hand;
He picks himself up, and brushes the dirt,
Dad checks him over, sure he's not hurt.

Penney Lang

Next out is Steve, on his own poddy calf,
Suddenly it stops, and the crowd start to laugh;
Holds on with one hand, the other in the air,
He's spurrin' that poddy, who's still standin' there.

With excited talk, you see this young pair,
The ride may be over, but the rush is still there;
Reliving their ride, on what they did do,
Giving advice, for next time they're through.

They're back being six, and playin' like a kid,
The little men inside them, are now truly hid;
Playing in the dirt, with their cars and their truck,
No longer worried, how to make that calf buck.

"See ya mate," one says to the other,
"I'm being called, I think it's me mother."
The spurs clink together, as he runs with each stride,
He'll be back next year, for the great Poddy Ride.

53

Outback Adventures

Working in outback Australia can be hazardous at times. Not only do officers have to find their way through extremely rough terrain to reach a patient, but they may also encounter wildlife, such as roos, moos and emus. Many an ambulance has come to grief from one of these encounters, and consequently spent quite some time off road at the panel beaters.

Some drivers swerve to miss the animal, while others suddenly apply the brakes hard. It is actually possible to screech the tyres on a dirt road, which is pretty impressive; however, this is not a good career move when you have the officer in charge in the back of the ambulance trying to treat a patient.

This was the case when a mother rushed her child to the ambulance station. As soon as she saw the paramedics, the distraught mother desperately told the officers that her child was choking.

Although the child was crying (indicating the airway wasn't completely blocked) the officers could see an object at the back of the child's throat. Without further delay, they loaded the mother and child in the back of the ambulance and headed for the hospital. The officer in charge, who was treating the patient in the back, had stood up to retrieve some equipment. At the same time, the driver suddenly hit the brakes. The sudden halt of the ambulance caused the officer in the back to lose his balance. As the officer became airborne, the mother caught a glimpse of his screwed-up face, and watched as his eyes and mouth opened wider as he flew past her and neared the driver's compartment.

Unfortunately, the flapping of his hands and arms didn't do much to soften his landing between the front seats.

As he and the vehicle came to a stop, the paramedic who had been driving looked down in surprise to see the officer in charge sprawled out on the floor, and wedged in between the two front seats beside him. The paramedic then asked, "Are you okay Boss?"
Dislodging himself from between the seats in the front compartment, the officer in charge gingerly got to his feet, and returned back to where he came from.

Thankfully, as a result of the sudden stop, the object in the child's mouth was also dislodged and consequently spat out by the patient.

A very relieved mother, however, couldn't stop giggling all the way to the hospital as she recalled the image of watching the officer fly past her, and the look of absolute horror etched on his face.

54

Country Music

A long way out of town on a country highway, paramedics, fire and police officers were busy attending to a driver involved in a truck rollover. With heads down and tails up, all were concentrating on treating and extricating the truckie who had rolled his vehicle into a cane field off the highway.

Suddenly a different sound interrupted the organized chaos that accompanies such incidents.

"What's that?" asked a fire officer, causing all chatter to stop.

"It sounds like classical music," somebody replied. "But where is it coming from?"

As the music grew louder, everyone at the crash scene stopped what they were doing. Like meerkats, their heads popped up one by one over the entangled wreck and the long cane stalks, to see something that didn't seem quite right.

With *Beethoven's Symphony No. 6* now filling the air, they found the sight before them hard to comprehend. The music belonged to none other than a leather-clad bikie, whose long beard was flapping in the wind against an open-faced black helmet. As he cruised past the accident scene on his motorbike, he gave a slight wave and continued on his way.

As the motorbike and music faded in the distance, one by one the officers' heads popped back down again and out of sight, as they resumed their previous positions and completed the job at hand.

55

Fine Talking

A woman and her daughter were driving from their country home to attend an event in a town near the city. While driving through one of the many towns on the way, the woman glanced up in the rear-view mirror and noticed what seemed to be an unmarked police car. Feeling smug, she said to herself, "I've got the car on cruise control, so I'm all right, they won't get me."

Suddenly her mobile phone rang. She recognized the ring tone was that of her husband. Picking up the handpiece and answering the phone, the woman engaged in a lengthy conversation with her husband. A few minutes into their conversation, the woman could hear the high-pitched sound of a siren. Thinking it was various sirens and acoustics belonging to her daughter's music, the woman proceeded in turning down the volume of the car stereo. However, the noise not only persisted but became louder.

At the other end of the line, her husband could hear the noise also and asked her,

"What's that noise I can hear in the background?"

"Yeah, I can hear it too, but I don't know where it's coming from."

At the same time she looked into the rear-view mirror to see red and blue flashing lights coming from the vehicle directly behind her.

"Oh, it looks like I'm being pulled over by the police, honey," she said in a surprised tone.

"Are you speeding?" inquired her husband.

"No, I've got it on cruise control. I wonder what they want?"

With the phone still to her ear, she used her elbow to activate the indicators and started to slow down. Pulling off to the shoulder of the road, she said to her husband, "Honey I'd better go now and see what the policeman wants. I'll ring you right back."

Winding down the window, the woman poked her head out.

"Is there anything wrong?" she asked, as the policeman walked up beside her car.

"Tell me you weren't talking on your mobile phone just now?" the policeman asked.

"Would you believe me if I said 'No'?"

"Not really," he said shaking his head. "May I see your driver's licence, please?"

Handing him her driver's licence, the policeman recognized that she was from out of town and inquired, "So how's the country these days?"

"Fine!" she gruffly replied, then thought to herself: Wish I was still there.

Even a bit of sweet-talking didn't save her from a fine and loss of points.

56

Outback Jack

This poem, written in September 2009, is in recognition of all those people who have made the outback their lives. They don't expect a lot from others and are quite content to live a simple and carefree life.

Penney Lang

Outback Jack

The old fella walks with a steady gait,
You'd never think he was sixty-eight;
His life is simple, come 'n sit back,
'Cause this is the tale of Outback Jack.

Born and raised out the back of Queensland,
He's lived all his life on this great southern land;
With his Akubra hat he'd walk a long mile,
And wherever he goes he wears a broad smile.

He worked the timber trade when young,
On his guitar, he likes to strum;
With rugged features and weathered hands,
Never seen the beach, or touched the white sands.

A sense of humor, he has, this 'ol guy,
Keep on your guard, for he can be sly;
He's hard to decipher, this is true,
But a true blue Aussie, through 'n through.

His pride and joy is Amber his horse,
Like any woman she's stubborn of course;
He keeps her watered and cuts her hay,
But he wouldn't have it any other way.

On holiday, this man has never been,
The sights of the world, he's never seen;
A flick of a button, the show unravels,
Through the TV, is how he travels.

173

Always friendly and stops for a chat,
He loves to scratch the ambo's cat;
A wave of his hand he says, "G'day,"
And heads to the pub at the end of the day.

A simple man with a simple life,
Never cared though to take a wife;
Doesn't ask for much, so give him a go,
You might be surprised 'bout this old bloke ya know.

The outback is full of people like this,
If I lived in the city it's something I'd miss;
No hustle and bustle or chimney stacks,
But simple living and Outback Jacks.

Penney Lang

Bits and
Pieces

Paramedics In Stitches

57

The Ripple Effect

When traumatic situations arise, people fall into three categories: The first category includes people who deal well with the situation at hand and then move on without a hitch. The second category includes people who deal with the situation initially, but then fall into a heap afterwards. And then there is the third category which includes people who suffer from what I call 'The Ripple Effect.' These people not only go to pieces regarding the situation, but soon find that they too have become a casualty and suffer side effects from what they see or smell. A good example of a ripple effect is when someone yawns. It doesn't take long before those around us, including ourselves, start to yawn.

While playing in the front yard of a lowset house, a boy, aged about fourteen, fell over and injured his right arm. Feeling an intense pain in his forearm, the boy concluded that it might be broken. After calling out to his mother, he sat on the grass cradling his injured arm.

On seeing his mother coming through the front door, the boy looked up at her saying,

"I think I've broken my arm, and I can't move my fingers."

Despite the absence of blood or any obvious

deformity to his arm, the boy's mother started to become lightheaded. Feeling like she was about to faint, she recognized the need to lie down immediately, even if it was in the middle of the concrete driveway.

"You'll have to ring the ambulance," she gasped. "They will know what to do."

With that, the boy got up and went inside to make the phone call.

While answering the emergency dispatcher's questions, the operator asked the boy if there was anybody with him.

"Yes," replied the boy. "My mum's just outside."

"Okay. Would I be able to speak to her please?" asked the dispatcher.

"Not really. She can't come to the phone because she's lying down outside on the driveway."

"Oh," replied the dispatcher. "Is she all right?"

"Yeah, she's okay. Mum just needed to lay down when I told her that I'd broken my arm, otherwise she would have fainted," stated the boy.

Sure enough, when the paramedics arrived, they found a woman sprawled out on the driveway with their young male patient sitting beside her, patting the hand of his pale mother with his uninjured hand saying, "It'll be all right, Mum."

58

Out of the Hearts of Babes

I had been asked to give a twenty minute talk to a group of forty children, all under eight years old. For me, the idea of talking to a group of under-eights was a little daunting. For a start, trying to keep them entertained during any time frame is a challenge within itself, especially when the ages range from three to seven years old.

Having not had any children of my own, I tried to imagine how much information these little ones could take in. I like to make these school visits fun and informative, hoping that I can share something important with them that they can take home—whether it's the emergency number or helping them understand some safety issues.

As the children were led onto the grassed area, I could already hear some keen fans serenading various siren sounds.

As soon as they were seated, I started off by asking, "Who has been for a ride in an ambulance?"

Before I'd finished the question, little hands were already waving in the air, eager to tell me about their own personal experience of riding in the ambulance.

One little boy about four years old, who was sitting nearby, suddenly stood up. I recognized him as the younger brother of a little girl I had recently transported to hospital. While we were treating his older sister, he had been very quiet the whole time, and I wasn't sure whether he understood what was going on.

A couple of days after I had taken his sister to hospital, the little boy's mother told me that he'd informed his entire kindergarten class, "Mum pulled my sister out of the shower and then she started shaking her because my sister wouldn't wake up. Then Mum called the police, and when the police came, they took Mum away!"

However, today he must have realized that it wasn't the police, but the ambulance who 'took his mum away.'

Standing up in front of everyone, he pointed to me and excitedly announced, "You took Mum, my sister and me for a ride in the ambulance!"

It's not often that we receive any thanks for the job we do—and we don't expect it either—but when we do, it can be really special. This little boy's sister had sent us a lovely 'thank you' card. Apparently she insisted that her mother send it before she had to go to another hospital for further tests.

Continuing on, I steered the conversation toward safety issues. To help them understand the necessity of wearing a helmet when riding a bicycle, I asked the group, "Why should a helmet be worn when riding a bicycle?"

One little boy replied, in a matter-of-fact tone, "If you don't wear your helmet, you'll fall off, hit your head and then they bury you in the ground."

Obviously somewhere, something had made quite

an impression on that little boy.

My next question was: "Does anyone think it is scary to go in the ambulance?"

One little girl piped up saying, "Yes, I think it is."

"Why do you say that?" I asked.

"Because, they take you away and then they steal you," she replied.

But the highlight of that day was the little boy, mentioned earlier, whose sister I had recently transported.

As the children started to crowd around me in an effort to line up and have a look in the ambulance, a little hand pushed its way through the crowd of children towards me. There in the little boy's hand was the smallest bunch of purple wildflowers I had ever been presented with. My heart just melted.

I can now understand, if ever so slightly, how a mother's heart melts when her own children present her with a flower, randomly picked from the garden—purely out of love.

59

Supermedic

When paramedics are placed on-call between shifts, they can still go about their daily business, as they aren't required to stay at home. However, the officer is required to be contactable for the entire period, and must be able to respond immediately. For example, the paramedic couldn't go anywhere where there wasn't a mobile phone signal or landline available. (This means that deep-sea diving or parachuting are probably out of the question).

Sometimes when you are going about your normal business, a call will come in at the most inopportune time. Such as the time when I'd just got in the shower and had my hair nicely lathered with shampoo. Responding to a call with soap suds still in your hair is not a good look!

With the limited freedom he had while on-call, Tim didn't want to be confined to his residence, especially when the weather was fantastic. Knowing that he would still have good mobile phone coverage, he decided to take his family to the beach.

Driving the ambulance, Tim followed his wife and children who were in the family car, and soon found a park under a shady tree in the parking lot near the surf lifesavers' clubhouse.

After several minutes of relaxing on the sand and listening to the gentle sound of the waves breaking on the shore, he was suddenly brought back to reality when his mobile phone rang. It was the communications centre requesting him to respond to an emergency.

Suddenly, Tim sprung into action and sprinted across the hot sand towards the ambulance.

Unlocking the side door of the ambulance, he dived inside and closed the door behind him. Less than a minute later, after quickly changing into his uniform, he emerged from the ambulance. Shutting the side door behind him he turned around to the sound of people clapping. A group of people had watched Tim sprint up the beach, dive into the ambulance and emerge like Superman (minus the cape, red boots and undies on the outside). After giving a little bow and duly thanking them, Tim ran around to the driver's side, hopped in and drove off to attend the emergency call.

So the next time you see a paramedic with soaking wet hair, or frantically running to the ambulance without shoes and socks on, chances are that he or she has been on-call and has had to drop everything at very short notice to attend an emergency call.

60

Fire! Fire!

Rule Number 1: Always make sure you have the facts right before making any rash decisions.

Rule Number 2: If in doubt, check for yourself and don't rely on someone else's word.

Any significant fire that may involve a building or threaten houses usually involves not only the Fire Service but also the ambulance and police.

Responding to a fire call on the outskirts of town brought the three services together. However, when they arrived at the address given to them by the communications centre, no fire could be found.

"I don't see any fire here," commented one fire officer.

"Looks like it might be a hoax call," mused another.

"I'm not sure, but we might have found our fire. Let's go and take a look over there," instructed the Fire Captain, as he pointed to a plume of black smoke billowing up into the sky in the near distance.

A convoy of emergency vehicles, consisting of two fire trucks, an ambulance (with a second unit on the way), and two police cars, meandered their way through the streets. As the procession continued, Beth called on the CB radio to Ross, who was in the second ambulance unit and quite a distance away from the other emergency vehicles.

"Ross, there's no fire at the address we were given. However, I'm following the fire trucks to a property just out of town." And she proceeded to give him a commentary of which streets they were travelling on.

As the vehicles neared the property where the smoke was coming from, Beth could see an elderly couple in the garden busily pruning their hedges, and throwing the offcuts on a fire in the garden.

At the sight of two fire trucks, an ambulance and two police cars pulling into their driveway, the elderly couple stood paralyzed with mouths agape, pruning shears held in mid-air and eyes transfixed on the sight before them. As they watched the front driveway of their property turn into an emergency services parking lot, the couple looked at each other, perplexed as to what the problem was.

The officers now alighted from their vehicles and walked up to the couple. Here, the fire chief went on to explain what had happened. As they all started to make light of the situation, a siren could be heard in the near distance.

"Oh no!" exclaimed Beth. "I forgot about Ross."

Suddenly, the second ambulance unit came roaring over the hill with lights and siren blaring. As the ambulance raced past the house, Ross looked over in time to see the other emergency vehicles assembled at the property he was about to go past. Screeching to a

186

halt, he then backed the ambulance up and parked it among the other vehicles. With the adrenaline still racing through his veins after the emergency run, Ross leapt out of the ambulance and bolted around the side of the house only to find a group of firemen, police officers and Beth laughing at him.

Doing a complete 360 degree spin in an attempt to survey the scene, he finally realized that the fire was coming from the garden clippings, heaped in the corner of the garden.

Eventually Ross's adrenaline rush subsided and the emergency crews climbed into their vehicles and headed back to their respective stations. Meanwhile, the elderly couple recommenced their gardening and continued to feed the fire.

61

When the Going gets Tough ...

You've heard of the saying: 'When the going gets tough, the tough get going'. Not so with some people. It's more like: 'When the going gets tough, the tough ... pretend to faint', and so enter the paramedics who get called to an unconscious collapse.

We respond to the call, on a Code One with lights and siren blaring through the night. (It's always at night, because these calls invariably include a party, alcohol and lots of people). As we turn down the street and approach the scene, we see half a dozen adolescents frantically waving us down as if we were going to drive straight past them. Tempting as that might be, we pull up at the kerb. We are then led through a throng of swaying, stubby-holding blokes and others pretending to be in need of mouth-to-mouth resuscitation, until we finally reach our patient.

After a quick assessment to rule out any life-threatening conditions, and quickly coming to the conclusion that our patient, for some unknown reason at this stage, is faking this unconscious episode, we load the patient onto the stretcher and into the ambulance.

Now this is my favorite part ...

Once the back door of the ambulance is closed, and our voices are no longer overpowered by the blaring music, I lean over to the patient and in a soft but stern voice say, "Okay, it's just you and me now in the back of the ambulance. Nobody else is here. What's happened?"

Miraculously their eyes start to flutter open. Moving their eyes from side to side, they start to focus in on their new surroundings. It is only now that they realize they are no longer in the situation they were in earlier. Sometimes a tear winds its way down their cheek, and they begin to fill me in on the details.

Unfortunately not everybody responds this way, and we go to the other end of the scale. One night Andrew and his partner were called to an unconscious male who was sprawled out in an ungainly fashion amongst mangroves near a creek.

When the paramedics reached the unconscious patient, they immediately applied a sternal rub (vigorous rubbing of the sternum with your knuckles), which roused the patient from his groggy state.

As the patient's conscious level improved, he sat up with a start and looked around to familiarize himself with his surroundings.

Suddenly, he leapt to his feet, started verbally abusing the paramedics and throwing punches in their direction. Realizing he wasn't getting anywhere with this display, he turned and started to sprint across the marshy ground.

Not wanting to be responsible for letting the patient go and then having to explain to the police why their patient was found 'floating in the nearby creek' the next day, Andrew set off in hot pursuit.

As he chased after their patient, Andrew began to lighten the load from his belt. First went the mobile phone and the torch, followed by the portable radio and anything else attached to his belt until nothing was left, leaving a trail of miscellaneous equipment strewn across the ground.

Having narrowed the gap and timed it just right, Andrew dived through the air. As he wrapped his arms around the patient's ankles, they both crashed to the ground in a heap. Unbeknown to Andrew though, he had crash tackled the patient onto a green ants' nest.

Jumping onto the patient and holding him down with his body weight, Andrew brought the patient's arm up over his back with one hand, and then grabbed a handful of the patient's jeans and jocks firmly with the other. Meanwhile Andrew's partner had called the police, who were not far from their location.

As the patient started to thrash around, mainly due to the ants biting him, Andrew, who was still oblivious to the ant situation, tightened his grip on the patient saying, "Right, you're gonna get up now."

As Andrew yanked him up from the ground, the patient's jocks stretched more than what Andrew thought they would, and ended up between the patient's shoulder blades, resulting in a huge and uncomfortable wedgie.

With the patient now up off the ground and on tiptoes, he started squealing, "They're biting me. They're biting me!"

Ignoring the patient's cries, Andrew frog-marched him back to where his partner and the ambulance were.

It wasn't until the two men were in the back of the ambulance and on their way to hospital, that Andrew now felt something biting *him*.

Under the fluorescent light, Andrew could now see a dozen or more green ants crawling over his arms and legs, not to mention the number that were on the patient, who by now was starting to come out in red lumps all over his body.

Meanwhile, another ambulance crew went back to the scene and picked up the gear
Andrew had left behind. Later, they met him at the hospital saying, "We managed to retrieve your gear without any problems. We could tell where you'd been."

62

A Sticky Situation

One Thursday afternoon we were called to a bus accident about twenty kilometres south of a small town.

A 4WD vehicle had collided with the rear of the local bus, which was returning from a shopping trip. There were about eight people on board, and all were elderly.

The only two ambulance vehicles we had left in town were dispatched, along with a crew from another station, which was just under an hour away.

As the driver of the 4WD was only shaken and didn't have any injuries, I proceeded across the road to the bus to assist my partner. Everybody was still on board, and my partner was assessing them for injuries.

As I boarded the bus, apart from groceries strewn all over the floor, I could see everybody had spots of white paint on them.

Apparently there was a ten litre drum of white acrylic paint situated in the back of the bus along with the groceries. Unfortunately the drum had split from the impact of the accident. Not only had it spray-painted the inside of the bus, but also everybody on board.

I then looked toward the back of the bus. There was Elsie, a little old lady who had suffered a stroke several years earlier, sitting silently in a wheelchair and staring straight ahead. She was covered from head to toe in thick white paint. There was so much of it on her that it looked like someone had poured the whole drum of paint over her head.

Due to the stroke, Elsie was unable to speak but I could just make out her pink lips and blinking eyes from under the paint, as it dripped from her hair and fingers. She looked quite a sight, but the shocked look on her face said it all!

Thank goodness nobody was seriously injured. After many showers, the hospital staff finally removed all of the paint from Elsie.

63

Mamma Maria

Arriving on-scene at a football club one evening, paramedics Luke and Lee were met by a number of Italian men and women dressed in formal attire. While one of the men informed Lee of what had happened, Luke was busily removing the primary response kit and other items from the ambulance.

The continuous beat of the music didn't seem to drown out the laughter and chatter coming from the football clubhouse situated on a hill overlooking the playing field. As they neared the building, Lee could make out what seemed to be an Italian wedding reception, with a number of people on the dance floor trying their best to perform various dance moves. Others mingled or sat around tables chatting and laughing with their friends.

The officers were guided through the crowded and noisy function room, down a narrow passageway lined with guests, to where an elderly woman was lying on the floor. The bride was kneeling on the floor with the elderly woman's head resting on her lap. As she gently stroked the elderly woman's hair from her forehead, the bride looked up with relief as the paramedics approached them.

The elderly woman explained to the paramedics

that she had slipped on the floor and landed awkwardly on her ankle. Confident that the patient had no other injuries, Lee continued to treat the woman for her ankle injury, while Luke went back to the ambulance to bring in the stretcher.

At this stage, quite a crowd had started to gather down the passageway and around the patient.

As the stretcher was manoeuvred down the passageway, the bride started to stand up to make way for the stretcher. In doing so, she became light-headed and gracefully fell back down onto the floor.

Luke raced over to the bride to assess her for any injury. Fortunately, she hadn't hurt herself but, as part of the assessment, Luke inquired as to what she thought might have caused her to feel light-headed.

Leaning toward the officer, she whispered, "I'm pregnant."

Luke's face suddenly beamed, and in a loud voice he cried out, "Pregnant! Oh how wonderful. Congratulations."

As quick as a wildfire spreading through a dry and parched country, the whispered words of, "Maria, she's pregnant," echoed down the passageway, followed by, "How embarrassing for the family."

Suddenly the music ground to a halt as someone cried out in an Italian accent: "No, no. This cannot be true!"

With that, the mother of the bride collapsed in a heap on the dance floor.

As the paramedics now assessed the mother of the bride, the father of the bride joined them. Through clenched teeth he warned, "You'd better stick around, 'cause when I catch up with that husband of hers, I'm gonna kill him!"

With three patients now loaded in the ambulance—the elderly woman, the bride and her mother—they began to make their way out of the football grounds and toward the hospital. However, not before witnessing a very frightened groom sprinting across the playing field being chased by the bride's brothers who were yelling and waving their arms furiously at him.

64

Mind your P's and Q's

Most healthcare professionals, including doctors, nurses and paramedics, are not superstitious. However, if you walk into an emergency department and say, "It's really *quiet* today," you will not only bring the entire room to a halt, with staff almost giving themselves whiplash from spinning around to identify the culprit, but you'll also receive a barrage of derogatory remarks, as they quickly usher you outside—mainly for your own safety.

You see, it seems that when one includes the 'q' word in the conversation when healthcare professionals are at work, it is inevitable that, sooner rather than later, the phone will ring and either the ambulance is sent to a case, or the emergency department is notified of a patient. Regardless of who is involved, by the end of the shift, things will have turned 'pear-shaped'.

One paramedic came up with the phrase, 'Less than frantic'. This seems to be accepted, just so long as the 'q' word is not mentioned.

If you are the mischievous type, want to see the reaction for yourself, it should be mentioned that doing so could be detrimental to your health. I recommend that you plan your escape route first, and make sure you can run really fast. If, on the other hand, you *are* a healthcare professional, you only say *the word* once your shift has finished and you're on your way out the door. But remember, you still have to come back for the next shift!

Some paramedics are not only careful to refrain from using the 'q' word, but they are also careful about the colour of underwear worn while on shift.

No, they aren't infatuated with undies, but it seems that if red-coloured underwear is worn, it can be guaranteed that you will be busy for the entire shift.

While attending a motor vehicle accident one day, Troy, the officer in charge, was heard asking his staff, "Okay, so who's wearing the red undies?"

Of course, none of the staff were game to own up.

On another particularly busy day, Troy and his partner Ray had been run off their feet attending another nasty motor vehicle accident. When they had finally arrived back at the station, Ray suddenly went pale.

As Troy inquired about his partner's health, Ray took him aside and whispered, "Troy, I've just realized. I think it's me who's caused us to be so busy today."

Taken aback, Troy asked, "What do you mean?"

"I'm wearing red undies!" Ray exclaimed.

As Troy let out a slight laugh Ray continued, "No! I'm serious mate. I'm wearing red undies. See," and proceeded to undo the top button and fly of his trousers revealing the offending red piece of material.

Seriously Now

65

Chicken Surprise

An intensive care paramedic had been sent to back up a crew of student intensive care paramedics who were attending to a near drowning at the beach. The male patient, who was allegedly intoxicated, had fallen into the ocean from a rocky outcrop which was a favourite area for fishermen.

Apparently some men who happened to be fishing nearby pulled the patient from the water and called for the ambulance.

When the crews arrived, the patient was unconscious but still had a pulse. However, his breathing was slow and quite shallow, and it appeared that his airway was almost blocked.

Using the laryngoscope and Magill's forceps for the first time, one student paramedic looked down the patient's throat and told his mentor, "I can see something white with a bit of pink around it, blocking the patient's airway."

"Well, should it be there or shouldn't it?" asked the intensive care paramedic.

"No. Anatomically it shouldn't," replied the student.

"Well get it out of the way then," instructed the senior officer.

Grabbing hold of the foreign object with the forceps and tugging at it, the student stated, "It's stuck, I can't get it out!"

"Well, considering it's a blocked airway, it's either anatomically supposed to be there or it's got to be removed so that we can clear the patient's airway."

Getting a firmer grip on the foreign object once again, the student gave it another good tug. Suddenly it broke free and as the foreign object was removed, the patient took a gasp of air.

Pulling the object out of the patient's mouth, the student threw it on the ground and exclaimed, "What on earth is that?"

On seeing a white piece of meat on the ground with a small amount of blood on the end of it, the intensive care paramedic suddenly gasped in horror saying, "You've pulled out his uvula!" (The fleshy tissue seen dangling above the tongue at the back of the throat.)

The poor student suddenly went pale and speechless. Feeling both his heart and stomach doing a flip, he thought to himself: How could I have pulled that out instead?

Noticing the absolute horror etched on his apprentice's face, the senior officer poked him in the ribs saying, "No, no, only joking mate." But the poor student was still in shock and couldn't utter a word.

Now that the patient was breathing on his own, the four paramedics carried him up the beach and into the waiting ambulance.

On arriving at the hospital, one of the paramedics immediately jumped out of the ambulance and raced into the resuscitation room of the emergency department, where the nurses and doctors were waiting for the patient's arrival. The paramedic then informed the nurse in charge of the joke the officers had played on their colleague.

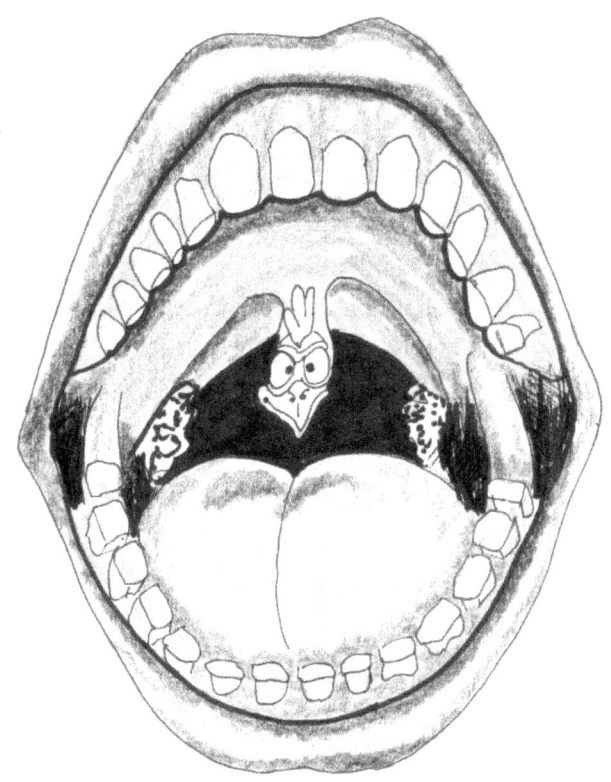

After the patient had been transferred to the hospital bed, the nurse in charge went outside to where the paramedics were busy tidying up their vehicle.

Holding an empty specimen jar, she turned to the student who was still in a slight state of shock, and said, "The anaesthetist has just arrived and noticed that the patient is missing his uvula. Do you happen to have it?"

Regaining his composure, the student gave a slight chuckle and looking at his colleagues, muttered something about finding somebody else's uvula for her. At this the nurse started laughing and walked back inside the hospital.

The foreign object that was pulled from the patient's throat, turned out to be a piece of chicken, obviously consumed prior to the accident.

The patient pulled through without any neurological deficits to once more enjoy eating chicken—with his uvula still intact. The student went on to successfully become a very competent intensive care paramedic who, to this day, still threatens to return the joke on an unsuspecting former mentor.

66

Skeleton Crew

It's amazing what you might see in the front seat of an ambulance at times. Trevor told me one day he had to deliver a first aid lecture to a group of people, and decided to take along 'Mr Bones' the skeleton.

Trevor was using an administration vehicle, which was often used for public education. Being a sedan, it wasn't capable of carrying a stretcher. Trevor now realized he had a slight problem as to how he would transport Mr Bones.

Problem solved. He sat 'the gentleman' in the front seat of his car, made sure he had a seatbelt on, and placed a cap on Mr Bone's head.

While stopped at a set of traffic lights, Trevor decided he would have some fun with the nearby motorists who were also waiting at the traffic lights.

It wasn't long before he got the reaction he was looking for. As Trevor proceeded to have quite a good 'conversation' with Mr Bones he couldn't help but notice the motorist on his left give a double-take. As the motorist stared at Mr Bones, a smile began to creep on his face. Recognising who Trevor's passenger was, he then nudged the passenger beside him. Trevor could now see the female passenger peer over the driver's shoulder and start to giggle.

The traffic lights then turned green and Trevor and Mr Bones drove off to meet their first-aid class.

67

Shocking Treatment

The strangest cardiac arrest case I ever attended came one Tuesday morning in October. We were dispatched to the medical centre where a female patient was experiencing chest pain.

Soon after we arrived, having set up our equipment and receiving a handover from the doctor, the patient suddenly went into cardiac arrest.

As soon as the electric current from the defibrillator hit the patient, she let out an almighty cry: "Ouch, that hurt!"

We all looked at each other in amazement, as people normally remain in an unconscious state.

Next, the rhythm on the cardiac monitor showed that the patient had once again arrested. Nil response, nil pulse and nil breathing. We charged up the defibrillator and zap!

"Oh I wish you wouldn't do that!" she begged.

Finally, after another episode of cardiac arrest, with the same spontaneous result, we loaded the patient in the ambulance to make the quick trip to hospital.

With the doctor in the back assisting my partner, the patient arrested twice on the way and again as we entered the doors to the coronary care unit. Following her eighth arrest, with subsequent defibrillation, the patient was transferred to a bed and handed over to the hospital staff.

A week later my partner and I visited the patient in hospital to see how she was recuperating following her heart surgery. After much discussion about her health, I asked her if she remembered any of the defibrillation shocks we gave her. She replied that she remembered one at the medical centre and the last one we gave on entering the coronary care unit, saying that she knew we had to give her the shocks, but she wished they didn't hurt so much.

68

Perfect Timing

It was New Year's Eve when a crew were sent to a male patient experiencing chest pain. After arriving on-scene and taking one look at the patient, Stan, who was the senior officer, instructed his junior partner, "We have to make a move with this patient, **NOW!**"

The patient didn't have very good odds to begin with. He was in his late sixties to early seventies, obese, a diabetic, and a paraplegic as a result from a motor vehicle accident many years ago.

After the ambulance officers started the appropriate treatment of drugs, oxygen, cardiac monitoring etc, the patient was placed on the stretcher in preparation for transport.

No sooner had they loaded him in the back of the ambulance than the patient looked up at Stan and muttered in a feeble voice, "I don't feel too well." With that, the patient went into cardiac arrest.

Stan quickly dropped the head of the stretcher, so that the patient was now lying on his back, which allowed the paramedics to place the defibrillation pads on his chest. Directly after a shock of 200 joules was delivered to the patient, Stan was on the two-way radio to the communications centre, notifying them of the situation, so that they in turn could notify the receiving hospital.

When the dispatching officer requested the patient's surname, Stan called out to his partner who was driving, and asked, "What's this bloke's name?"

Before his partner could reply, a faint voice came from the direction of the stretcher and answered, "Wilson."

69

Booby Traps

There was a time when the control supervisor would be working on his own from midnight until about seven o'clock in the morning.

The control centre was on the same grounds as the ambulance station. During the evening, when it was 'less than frantic', the officers on shift would walk over to the control centre and have a chat with the supervisor. This was mainly around midnight when the dispatching officer, who had worked until midnight, had gone home.

One night when all the crews were out on cases, somebody broke into the ambulance station.

The next night an officer from the ambulance station wandered over to the control centre, as per usual at midnight, to have a chat with the supervisor. No sooner had he opened the door, than there was a sudden clanging and banging noise, with pots and pans coming down over the poor unsuspecting officer.

Ducking for cover the officer exclaimed, "What's going on?"

The supervisor had decided to set up his own booby traps in case the thief decided to return.

For many years, while the supervisors worked on their own, it became common knowledge to either let this particular supervisor know you were going to visit him, or risk walking into his booby traps. If you forgot, you only forgot once.

70

Funny Faces

Many Emergency Services employ the 'Trauma Teddy' which is given to children to comfort them during a traumatic event. At times when this has not been on hand, improvisation has come to the fore with paramedics using the 'Glove Balloon.'

It's simply a surgical glove blown up so that the fingers resemble a spiked hairdo, and the thumb is the nose, with a smiley face drawn around it (depending on how artistic the paramedic is). This sometimes brings the desired effect for the duration of treatment, until a more permanent toy is found.

Some paramedics have gone one step further. Pulling the glove over the top of their head, they have mastered the art of blowing the glove up with the air coming from their nose. This is quite an impressive display.

After placing the glove over their head they then pull it down until it covers their nose. The glove is now inflated by blowing it up with the air coming from their nostrils. It now resembles a rooster's comb on top of their heads. Think it can't be done? Think again!

In fact, I heard that a certain motorist was having a particularly bad day when he happened to pull up beside an ambulance at a set of traffic lights.

As the motorist looked outside his window he saw Gary sitting in the passenger seat of the ambulance. Facing toward the window, Gary pulled the glove down over his face, distorting it, and proceeded to blow the glove up with the air coming from his nostrils. With each blow, the 'rooster's comb' started to rise high on his head.

Next day, the same motorist went out of his way to thank Gary for brightening up his bad day. As he pulled up at the front of the ambulance station, the man saw Gary and his colleague hitting something across the bonnet of the ambulance. As the motorist got closer he realized the object they were hitting looked familiar. Here was Gary's 'rooster's comb' from the previous day, now turned into a glove balloon with a big smiley face drawn on it.

71

A Really Big Boy

One of the first things you learn when dealing with spinal cord injuries, apart from the obvious signs and symptoms such as pain, numbness or paralysis, is that males may develop an additional indication called a priapism.

Priapism is when a persistent abnormal erection occurs in the presence of an injury to the spinal cord. This may or may not be apparent initially but discreetness and modesty are obviously required when assessing for such a sign.

Some officers have a bit of trouble in displaying these qualities and open their mouths before they can put their brain into gear. Mike was one of these officers.

Approaching a scene where a motorcyclist had collided with another vehicle, the paramedics could see a male patient clothed in a t-shirt, boxer shorts and wearing thongs, lying in the middle of the road with his helmet still on.

After assessing the patient for injuries and removing his helmet, they found that the only apparent injuries were multiple abrasions from head to toe. But then Mike noticed the patient had a distinctive bulge, indicating the man had a possible priapism.

After explaining to the patient the need for him to

take a look to confirm this diagnosis, Mike discreetly peered down the man's boxer shorts.

Shaking his head he announced, so that all in earshot could hear, "Nope, there's no problem here."

Then turning to the patient Mike stated as a matter of fact, "You're just a REALLY BIG boy, aren't ya mate!"

72

Trust me, I'm a Professional

I have always had this saying: "To be professional, you have to look professional." This includes not only our uniform's appearance and the clean and tidy state of the ambulance cabin between jobs but, more importantly, what you are doing while treating a patient.

It's always been a common theory that whenever a person looks busy doing all sorts of things at once, people perceive that the *officer must know what they are doing*. This also includes the amount of mess created while engaging in something *really important*. (My mother can attest to the degree of mayhem I used to make in the kitchen).

Sadly though, things haven't changed that much, and the mess has only moved from the kitchen to the back of the ambulance. The underlying thought is: the messier the rear compartment of the ambulance, the more people are convinced that the officer has done a great job. That's my theory and I'm sticking to it.

As a mentor to student ambulance officers, I enjoy helping others increase their knowledge and seeing them progress. It's always satisfying to know that I have made a difference in that person's career and somehow am responsible for passing on a particular skill or a quality that they can aspire to.

In the case of one student, Dean, the skill for which I had sole responsibility of passing on, was the ability to make the back of an ambulance look like Cyclone Tracy[1] had made a short stopover. Although Dean has tried quite hard to impress me at times with the state of the ambulance after he's been in the back, I'm afraid I still hold the title, even if it was quite by accident.

The patient's condition was quite stable and a moderate amount of mess had been created, to verify that we had given the appropriate treatment. On arrival at the hospital, I went to move the drug kit out of the way. Not realizing that the kit wasn't shut properly, I grabbed hold of the handle and quickly pulled the kit up from the floor, only to have the contents explode throughout the cabin.

Together with the mess I had initially created, the entire floor cabin was now littered with syringes, needles, ampoules and dressings. The overall impression was that *something bigger than Tracy had been here*. As all the contents from the kit started to settle, Dean opened the back door of the ambulance.

I looked at Dean and immediately saw his eyes grow wide with envy at the sight before him. As a smile slowly crept onto his face, I could see that he was suitably impressed. He slowly shook his head from side to side saying, "Awesome! That's … just … awesome."

---

[1] Cyclone Tracy was a tropical cyclone that devastated the city of Darwin, Northern Territory, Australia, from Christmas Eve to Christmas Day, 1974.

This has now become a long-lasting goal for Dean. He views this as a competition and I believe to this day he is still trying to beat my record.

He mentions this when working with new partners who are embarrassed if they happen to leave a bandage on the floor. Dean just replies with a laugh and tells them, "That's nothing, the best mess maker I've ever seen in my career so far was my original mentor … " and proceeds to fill them in.

Professional indeed!

About the Author

Penney Lang (nee Trinder) was born in Brisbane, growing up on the north side. At the age of ten she moved with her family, including younger sister Alicia, to the Sunshine Coast.

After completing (Year 12), she became involved in the State Emergency Service and St John Ambulance Australia, Combined Division, on the Sunshine Coast. From these voluntary organisations, Penney's desire to help people was encouraged further, and she became an Honorary Ambulance Officer in 1991. After gaining full-time employment with the Ambulance Service, she graduated as a Qualified Ambulance Officer in 1995. Penney then furthered her skills and qualified to her current level as an Advanced Care Paramedic in the year 2000.

On 8 July 1996, Penney and several of her colleagues were awarded an Assistant Commissioner's Commendation for outstanding courage, dedication and professionalism exhibited during the Black Hawk tragedy[1] in Townsville on 12 June 1996.

That same year, she teamed up with a colleague and entered into the Institute of Ambulance Officers Australia competition where, on winning the regional competition, they competed as finalists in the state

---

[1] The Black Hawk tragedy was the mid-air collision between two Black Hawk helicopters during a training exercise near Townsville, in which 18 servicemen from the 5th Aviation Regiment and the Special Air Service Regiment were killed and another 12 were injured.

competition. She was awarded an Emergency Services Australia Day Medal in 1997.

Penney, who married her paramedic husband in 1996, has lived and worked throughout the state of Queensland.

This book came about from her own experiences, and from listening to various humorous tales told by her colleagues, who would often say: "Someone should write these stories down". In order to keep a record of these events, Penney decided to compile them into a series of short stories, while maintaining confidentiality at the same time. This is her first book.

Paramedics In Stitches